She looke____ _____ _ace with thos____ __ green eyes—her gaze not veering from his—and his world tilted.

It didn't just tilt but went whirling off its axis.

When he'd betrayed Eve four years ago, he'd broken his own heart. He'd known that was what he was doing at the time, but it hadn't stopped him.

If he stayed here, he'd be in danger of breaking his heart again.

His mouth dried and his heart pumped so hard he could barely draw breath. His immediate instinct was to flee. To get the hell out of Dodge before he managed to annihilate all of his hard-won peace of mind.

Peace of mind?

Ha! He didn't have any of that. He didn't deserve any of that. But he'd learned to live with what he'd done. To open that wound again...

His hands clenched. If he could make things right now, though? Maybe then he'd earn a measure of peace. He craved that, a sense of redemption—it was an ache in his soul.

Dear Reader,

There's something about a reunion story that grabs me in a way no other story can. I think it's due to all of the history that exists between the heroine and hero—it just...*simmers* in the background every time they're on the page together. It's the knowledge that these two people loved each other wholeheartedly in the past and that something terrible happened to tear them apart.

Eve and Damon have a fraught history, but there's something heroic in Damon's efforts to make amends when his and Eve's paths cross again. He has zero expectations of the woman he once loved. He is just determined to make her life better rather than worse. Can you tell that Damon was a dream to write? :)

Redemption of the Maverick Millionaire has three elements I adore—a heroine who has rebuilt her life and will do whatever she can to safeguard it, a glorious beach setting and a community to die for. I hope you enjoy your visit to Eve's town of Mirror Glass Bay and that this story puts a big dreamy smile on your face like it did for me.

Hugs and happy reading!

Michelle

Redemption of the Maverick Millionaire

Michelle Douglas

HARLEQUIN

Romance

ISBN-13: 978-1-335-55627-1

Redemption of the Maverick Millionaire

Copyright © 2020 by Michelle Douglas

This edition published by arrangement with Harlequin Books S.A.

For questions and comments about the quality of this book,
please contact us at CustomerService@Harlequin.com.

Harlequin Enterprises ULC
22 Adelaide St. West, 40th Floor
Toronto, Ontario M5H 4E3, Canada
www.Harlequin.com

Printed in U.S.A.

Michelle Douglas has been writing for Harlequin since 2007 and believes she has the best job in the world. She lives in a leafy suburb of Newcastle, on Australia's east coast, with her own romantic hero, a house full of dust and books, and an eclectic collection of '60s and '70s vinyl. She loves to hear from readers and can be contacted via her website, michelle-douglas.com.

Books by Michelle Douglas

Harlequin Romance

The Vineyards of Calanetti

Reunited by a Baby Secret

Snowbound Surprise for the Billionaire
The Millionaire and the Maid
A Deal to Mend Their Marriage
An Unlikely Bride for the Billionaire
The Spanish Tycoon's Takeover
Sarah and the Secret Sheikh
A Baby in His In-Tray
The Million Pound Marriage Deal
Miss Prim's Greek Island Fling
The Maid, the Millionaire and the Baby

Visit the Author Profile page
at Harlequin.com for more titles.

To the Lucas crowd, past and present—for the street parties, the chats over the front or back fences, the eggs and the all-around general neighborliness.

Praise for
Michelle Douglas

CHAPTER ONE

THE PHONE IN the top pocket of Damon Macy's pristine white business shirt vibrated. He pulled it out and gave it a cursory glance. A text with an email link and then a message.

You need to read this.

What the hell was Clay thinking, sending him anything today? He slipped the phone back into his pocket. *Later.*

His phone vibrated again but he ignored it. Darrell, his driver, as if sensing his employer's impatience, glanced in the rear-view mirror. 'Your flight is on time, Mr Macy. We'll reach Sydney airport in another four minutes. There will be an airline official waiting to escort you to your seat.'

'Thank you, Darrell.'

His damn phone vibrated again. For pity's sake, Clay knew he was off to clinch one of the biggest deals of his career. He'd been working on this deal for a solid eight months. It would cement him and his company—Macy Holdings—in the big league for good. He had no time for distractions.

He pulled his phone out again.

YOU REALLY NEED TO READ THIS!!!!!!

He blinked at the capitals and the line of exclamation marks that followed. Clay wouldn't be contacting him now unless he thought Damon needed to know whatever that website link had to tell him. His best friend was always lecturing him that he needed to stop and smell the flowers, but he'd never undermine Damon's work or aspirations—he knew how important this deal was.

'You have two minutes, Clay,' he murmured, clicking on the link.

A newspaper headline loaded on his screen. He stared at it.

Mirror Glass Bay residents outraged at new development!

Every muscle stiffened.

Mirror Glass Bay?

She lived in Mirror Glass Bay. He leaned forward to read the newsprint more quickly. *She'd* moved there and had built an entirely new life for herself after he'd…

He pressed a hand to his forehead, acid burning in his gut as he pushed that thought away and scanned the article. There was no reference to an Eve Clark. Not that he expected one. She'd worked hard to maintain a low profile.

According to the article, a new luxury beachside resort was being built in Mirror Glass Bay—less than a seven-minute walk from her beachside motel. His knuckles whitened about his phone. A brand-spanking-new resort had the potential to destroy her business.

He tried to still the churning in his gut. He owed that woman. And here was an opportunity to finally make amends—an opportunity for which he'd been waiting four long years.

She said she never wanted to clap eyes on you again.

His heart pounded. Hard. As if it were punishing him for the choices he'd made four years ago. The edges of his vision darkened and it took three breaths before he could ease the vice-like grip that tried to crush his lungs.

He would never hurt her again. *Ever.* But she didn't have to *clap eyes* on him—he could make sure that didn't happen. Regardless of how his every atom ached to catch the smallest glimpse of her.

'We're here, sir.'

He snapped to at Darrell's words. Owen, his VP, who had preceded him to the airport, had opened the car door and was waiting for his boss to emerge.

'Change of plan, Owen,' he said, exiting in one smooth movement, although internally things burned, rocked and crashed. Damon had learned early on never to reveal internal turmoil—a skill that had held him in good stead in the piranha-infested waters of the corporate world.

'Damon?'

'You're going to Frankfurt without me.'

Owen's mouth worked but no sound came out. With a visible effort, he reined in his shock. 'You are planning to be there, though? I mean—'

'Of course,' he cut in, irritable with his VP's shock, even though it was perfectly justified. 'This is nothing more than a minor delay.'

His second-in-command straightened with a nod, all brisk efficiency again. 'When will you arrive?'

Damon's mind flashed to the newspaper article. Greamsman Industries Pty Ltd was behind the development. His lips twisted. He and Kevin Greamsman had history. 'I'll aim to fly out tomorrow.' He bit back an oath. 'But in all likelihood I won't get away until Wednesday.' The timing couldn't be worse.

'Negotiations are expected to proceed the day we arrive.' Owen's colour came and went. 'Herr Mueller is going to be…disappointed.'

Herr Mueller would take it as a personal affront. They both knew that. 'Thank you for pointing out the obvious.'

His VP had the grace to look shamefaced.

'I'm not expecting you to perform miracles, Owen. Just concentrate on smoothing things over as well as you can until I get there.'

'Got it,' the other man said with a lamentable lack of enthusiasm.

He forced a weary severity to his voice. 'This is what I pay you the big bucks for. If you're not up for it, there are at least five other candidates who'd snap my arm off for the opportunity, and—'

'I'm definitely up for it,' Owen assured him with what should've been gratifying haste. 'You took me by surprise, that's all.'

Damon had taken himself by surprise; he was risking eight months' worth of hard work.

You owe her.

'I'll take care of Herr Mueller. You have my word.'

He clapped his VP on the shoulder. 'Good man.'

Damon turned to the airline executive who stood waiting nearby. Until this moment, he'd never particularly regretted not owning his own private jet. It had always seemed such an unnecessary indulgence.

Until today.

He consoled himself with the thought that, if he closed this deal with Herr Mueller, he could buy a whole fleet of jets if he wanted.

'I need to get to Byron Bay. Can you organise a charter for me?'

The airline executive gave a nod, pulled a phone from her pocket and began making the arrangements.

'Is there anything I need to know?' Owen hesitated. 'About Byron Bay?'

Damon shook his head. 'This is personal, I'm afraid. Not business.'

'Roger.'

A moment later another airline official appeared and gestured for Owen to follow him. The two men said cursory farewells and Damon's steward led him to a private luxury lounge. 'We should have you in Byron Bay by four o'clock, Mr Macy.'

Damon glanced at his watch. That was nearly four hours away.

'Joshua at the bar will organise any refreshments that you need. Let him know what you want and if you require use of the business centre. In the meantime, can I get you a drink?'

'Coffee—hot, black and strong.' He hit speed dial for his PA's number. 'I'd appreciate it if Joshua could keep it coming.' He needed his wits sharp and honed. He pressed his phone to his ear. 'Philip, I need you to find out everything you can about the new Greamsman development that's about to start in Mirror Glass Bay. And I need it yesterday.'

'Onto it,' Philip said without hesitation.

* * *

'You want to what?'

Kevin Greamsman leaned across the table in the boardroom of one of Byron Bay's most exclusive hotels to stare at Damon with an exaggerated lift of his eyebrows.

Damon shifted his gaze from his competitor's face to the view out of the window. The boardroom boasted a comprehensive view of the coastline. Numerous travel magazines and tourist boards had voted Byron Bay one of the most beautiful beaches in the world. Damon stared out at it with impassive eyes. They were right— it was magnificent.

But he didn't care about the view. He cared about the deal.

He shifted back to Greamsman. 'I want to buy you out,' he repeated. Mirror Glass Bay was a thirty-minute drive from Byron Bay and, from all accounts, sleepy. Where Byron Bay thrived on tourism, Mirror Glass Bay was doing its best to preserve its 'off the beaten track' tranquillity. While apparently beautiful, Mirror Glass Bay lacked Byron's colour, sophistication and the ultra-hippy surf vibe that brought tourists flocking from all corners of the globe.

The older man's eyes narrowed. 'I don't like you, Demon, and I don't like your tactics. What do you know that I don't?'

He used the nickname many in the industry

called Damon behind his back, but few had the courage to use it to his face. 'You don't have to like me, Greamsman. I keep telling you—this is business, not personal.'

Though he knew Greamsman wouldn't believe him. He was convinced Damon had used underhand tactics to win two recent government tenders. He no doubt now thought Damon had an inside track on some piece of news that would change the complexion of a development in Mirror Glass Bay in a more favourable way.

Rather than playing games or trying to field questions, he chose to be honest with the other man. 'I find myself becoming sentimental in my old age.' Old? He was only thirty-two, though most days he felt closer to sixty. 'I want to preserve Mirror Glass Bay's natural beauty, its sleepy nature. There's enough development and progress happening here in Byron and further north on the Gold Coast. It's not unreasonable for developers to be asked to leave some places unspoiled.'

'I don't believe you.'

But Greamsman's posture told Damon the opposite. It told him he did believe him and was trying to work out how to take advantage of it.

'I know how much you paid for the site. A little preliminary research shows me there are another two sites in the area that would meet the requirements of the luxury development you're planning. I'm prepared to offer you a fair price for the land.' He wrote a number down and pushed it across the table.

For a gut-wrenching moment he thought Kevin might push it back without even looking at it, shoot to his feet and tell him to go to the blazes just because he could. Damon had risen to the top for his ability to read people, and he could read that impulse clearly in the face of the man opposite. Kevin wanted to tell him that karma was a bitch; he wanted to march out of this boardroom feeling that he'd got the better of Damon.

But that warred with a second impulse—curiosity. When Kevin reached over to turn the slip of paper towards him, Damon knew curiosity had won out. The older man's eyebrows rose. 'This is actually a fair price.'

'I've already told you I'm not playing games.'

'And yet I find myself recalling the sting of having lost out on the container ship contract and find myself unmoved by this particular offer. Though, perhaps another two hundred thousand dollars might help.'

Damon had already factored that in—knowing Kevin would up the price—but he didn't betray that by so much as a flickering eyelash. 'I'm sure that could be arranged.'

'And I'm not signing that site over to you unless you sign a non-compete clause. I'm not handing over a piece of prime real estate just begging for development for you to then go and build your own luxury resort. I don't trust you, Demon.'

'You have yourself a deal, but only on the proviso you can have your man draw up the papers and send them to me for review before the close of business today,' he said, refusing to betray how much he hated that nickname.

Greamsman glanced to the man on his left, who nodded, before rising and sticking out his hand. 'Done. I'll meet you back here in the morning—nine on the dot—to sign the papers.'

Damon refused to let his satisfaction show. 'Till then.'

The papers were signed and the deal was done by nine-fifteen the next morning.

Kevin eased back, lacing his fingers over his stomach. 'You want to tell me what you're really up to now?'

Damon sipped the coffee Kevin had been good enough to provide, relishing the rich heat and full flavour. For the first time in two days he could finally taste something. Nerves had kept him screwed up too tight. He hadn't wanted to fail Eve. Not again.

Not that she'd ever know about this, of course.

He glanced out of the window at the beach and the sun, at the golden sand and an emerald sea. Would there be time to take a walk on the beach before he left, to dig his toes into the sand?

He shook off the thought. What was he thinking? He needed to get to Frankfurt without delay—had to try and salvage the situation with Herr Mueller who was, from all accounts, far from impressed.

'I had no hidden agenda. I told you the truth.'

'In that case, you should've waited another couple of days, Demon.'

The nickname made his back molars clench.

'Your haste surprised me. It was out of character. And you usually do far more due diligence before embarking on a deal of this magnitude.'

This deal had been far from usual, though, and the other man's words made his gut clench. What had he overlooked? Where had he gone wrong?

'I confess, I enjoyed taking advantage of your…recklessness.'

Kevin rubbed his hands together as if enjoying a great joke at Damon's expense. Ice tripped down Damon's back. What the hell had he missed?

'I can't say I'm sorry for it, though.' Kevin chortled some more. 'Nothing personal, Demon, you understand? It's just business, right?'

Damon calmly sipped his coffee, though his stomach had started to rebel. 'Want to let me in on the joke?'

'That piece of prime real estate you just bought is about to be slapped with an environmental injunction. It appears that it's a breeding ground for some rare seabird. I was walking away from the project—was chalking it up to experience. Instead, I made a killing. At Demon Macy's expense, no less.' He slapped the table and let loose a belly laugh that had his second chin wobbling. 'You win some and you lose some—I believe that's what you said to me last time we did business. I have to say, it's a joy to see you on the losing side for once.'

The hard knot in Damon's stomach eased. 'I got what I came for, Kevin.' Mirror Glass Bay and Eve's business were safe, and he had every intention of keeping them that way. 'Now, if you'll excuse me, I have a plane to catch.'

He turned away to stash the papers he'd just signed into his briefcase when the door to the boardroom crashed open.

'Mr Greamsman,' a female voice said, cutting through the air. 'Is it true you've just pulled out of your resort development?'

A *familiar* female voice. Damon closed his eyes and bit back an oath. *Eve!* He hadn't meant for her to see him, or even to know he'd been here. He'd resisted every bitter impulse yesterday to turn his hire car in the direction of Mirror Glass Bay just to see the place she called home. It took all his strength now not to swing around and feast his eyes on her.

'You're well informed, Ms Clark. Let me introduce you to Damon Macy, who has just bought the development site. I'm afraid I'll be moving my operations elsewhere.'

Two beats passed. 'Damon… *Macy*?'

He counted to five to give her a chance to gather herself—*five, four, three, two…* He turned, met her gaze and froze.

She wasn't wearing make-up. It seemed the most inane of things to notice, but when she'd worked for Spellman and Spelman she'd never walked through the office doors, let alone attended a business meeting, without her armour, a full face of make-up. He didn't know what it meant.

He opened his mouth but snapped it shut again. What was he going to say—*you're not wearing make-up? Looking good, Evie? Can I kiss you?* All of them were totally inappropriate.

And her white-faced shock tore him to the centre of his being. He'd known she never wanted to see him again, but to be presented with such stark evidence made him feel physically sick.

Her familiarity, though, punched through him in a way he hadn't expected, rocking him to his foundations. He hadn't known he had anything left inside him that could still *want*. And he wanted her with a ferocity that had only increased in the four years since he'd last seen her.

He wanted to throw his head back and roar against the unfairness of it.

Only it wasn't unfair, was it? This woman had

every reason to loathe him. And she did—he could see that in the endless depths of her green eyes—eyes the colour of sea glass. Some would call it poetic justice.

He'd call it hell. But it was a hell he deserved.

He swallowed and nodded. 'Hello, Eve.'

Greamsman glanced from one to the other, speculation rife in his eyes. 'You know each other?'

Her eyes turned hard and cold, her lips refusing to lift into anything even approximating a smile. '"Know" would be an exaggeration, Mr Greamsman.'

I thought I knew you, but I was wrong.

Her words from four years ago circled through his mind now. His temples started to throb.

'I once had the pleasure…' the word dripped with sarcasm '…of working with Mr Macy.'

'Ah, so you'll be aware of his business practices, then.'

That made his back stiffen. 'My business practices are completely above board. If they weren't, you'd have found a way to have my company brought before an industrial tribunal by now, Greamsman.'

'Perhaps, perhaps not,' the other man said. 'But your tactics…'

'Can leave a lot to be desired,' Eve finished, folding her arms.

'Well, my dear—'

'Don't call me your dear.' Cold eyes turned to his rival and Damon's spine unhitched a fraction with the relief of being released from their cold, penetrating knowingness and the accusation that flared in their depths.

'Yes, well,' Kevin blustered. 'If you'll excuse me, I have a plane to catch.' He gathered up his things before shooting Damon a malicious smile. 'Nothing personal, remember, Demon. Just business.'

Damon wanted to slam a fist into the other man's face—not for the smugness or his ridiculous game of one-upmanship but for continuing to call him that hideous nickname. The impulse made him suck in a breath. For the last four years he'd been incarcerated in some icy, contained world of his own. But one look at Eve had brought all those walls crashing down. Really?

He rolled his shoulders. It felt good, invigorating. Disturbing, too, but...he felt alive again. He straightened. When had he started to feel so dead inside?

He glanced at Eve as Greamsman and the lawyer left the room. She hated him, and he deserved her resentment, her censure, her mistrust—it was an undeniable truth. But he wanted to live again, to feel alive again. He was through with punishing himself. He'd done her the good turn she deserved. Now he was free to go to Frankfurt, do all he could to close the Mueller deal and then...

He lifted his chin. And then he'd take a holiday, walk on a beach somewhere and rethink his life…make some changes.

Her arms were still folded and the fingers of her right hand drummed against her left upper arm. She stuck out a hip and raised an eyebrow. He nodded. Before he could do any of that, he needed to deal with the here and now. 'I know you must hate me, Eve.'

She waved that away. 'Ancient history.'

He tried to gauge what was happening behind her eyes, but he couldn't. Had she really moved on so easily? A dark heaviness settled over him that he tried to shake off. He hoped she had.

'Is it true that you've bought the site from Greamsman?'

She didn't want to talk about the past. Her gaze was firmly fixed on the future—on her livelihood—as it should be. He pulled himself into straight lines and nodded. 'Yes.'

Her eyes didn't waver from his. That was one of the things he'd always loved about her—her unflinching strength.

'And what do you mean to do with it?'

The tightness in his chest started to drain away. Finally, he could give her something of worth. 'Absolutely nothing.'

She blinked as if his words made no sense.

'Mirror Glass Bay will retain its unspoilt character, preserved for generations to come as it should be. I know how special—'

'You're *not* going to build a big, shiny new resort on that spot?' she interrupted him.

'No, I'm not.' He waited for her shock to dissolve into relief...to dissolve into happiness. He didn't expect her to thank him, but one small smile didn't seem too much to ask for.

Her hands clenched and her face twisted. A breath shot out of her lungs and it seemed to leave her diminished, lesser...broken. 'What the hell did I ever do to you to deserve this? From you of all people!'

His mouth went dry. 'What are you talking about?'

She slammed a hand down to the table between them and eyed the pens, the bowls of mints and the coffee mugs as if she was trying to decide which of them to hurl at him first. 'Damn you, *Demon*.'

His jaw clenched so hard pain shot down his neck.

'Mirror Glass Bay *needed* that development.' What the hell...?

'You *wanted* that development?'

'*Yes!*'

He took a step back, his veins freezing to ice. Damn it all to hell, how had he got this so wrong?

Eve fell into a seat at the board table and dropped her head to her hands. She'd promised everyone to do her best. *Think!* She had to find a way to fix this. She was an intelligent woman. Her hands clenched into fists at her temples. She should be able to fix this. If she could only get her mind to work.

Except her mind had downed tools at the first sight of Damon.

'Eve?'

Damon's hand came into view and she jerked away. 'Don't touch me!'

He pulled his hand back, his face going white and the lines about his mouth pinching as if he were fighting a spasm of pain. Maybe he had a bad back, or a raging migraine. She really hoped so.

Her reaction to him had never been measured, but the ferocity of her animosity now took her off guard. It was just…

She'd never expected to see him again.

She'd never *wanted* to see him again.

'You *wanted* the development to go through?' he repeated.

'Yes!' The word snapped out of her, full of fire and brimstone, but she couldn't seem to moderate her tone.

'But there was a newspaper article that said local residents were against it.'

She stood, her entire body starting to shake. 'Are you telling me your research of what the residents of Mirror Glass Bay wanted was based on one newspaper article?'

His Adam's apple bobbed as he swallowed. 'I researched the development.' His Adam's apple bobbed again. 'Thoroughly.'

'*One* newspaper article?' she repeated, refusing to let the strong column of his throat distract her.

'The development was slotted for a resort. For holidaymakers. It would've been in direct competition to your motel.'

But his voice wavered as he uttered the words, and she couldn't believe what she was hearing. Had he done no research on Mirror Glass Bay—on her gorgeous, quirky and utterly frustrating community—at all? 'Not in competition,' she managed through gritted teeth. 'We'd have attracted completely different clienteles. The people who come to stay in my motel would no sooner think of staying in a luxury resort than they would take annual trips to Europe.'

He dragged a hand down his face and swore.

'Why?' She tried not to shout the word. 'Why did you get involved at all? Why did you have to meddle?'

'I wanted to make amends.' His lips pressed into a straight, uncompromising line, but he'd lost his colour and it hadn't come back yet. He looked as if he might throw up. She ignored the stupid skip of her heart, its stupid weakening. 'To you,' he croaked. 'I wanted to make amends to you. I wanted to help.'

She folded her arms across her chest so tightly they started to ache. She would *not* let his words warm her. She wouldn't even let herself believe them. 'If you wanted to help, why didn't you ask me first instead of going off half-cocked and ruining everything?'

He opened his mouth as if to protest but shut it again with a snap and a nod.

'Why couldn't you have left me alone? What the hell did I ever do to you to deserve…?'

She broke off, appalled at how heavily she breathed. It was as if she'd been running a race as hard and as fast as she could but still couldn't win…couldn't even seem to make it to the finish line. She hitched up her chin, desperately wanting to channel ice-cold composure. 'This has nothing to do with me, has it? It's about you wanting to allay a guilty conscience.'

'Maybe they're different sides of the same coin.'

'And maybe they're not. One is selfish and self-interested and the other isn't. We both know unselfishness isn't a trait you're known for.' She wanted to call him Demon again, but she didn't have the heart for it. 'Either way, looks like I'm the one having to pay the price. *Again.*'

'I can fix this, Eve.'

She didn't want him to. She wanted him out of her life for good. She never wanted to see him again.

Except…

She swallowed. It left her throat feeling bruised and sore. Except she'd promised her community, her friends, to do everything she could to make sure this resort went through. And she'd keep that promise, regardless of her animosity…regardless of the pain crushing her chest, as if seeing him now was breaking her heart all over again.

'I swear to you that I can fix this.' He sat at the table and pulled a pad and pen towards him. She remembered then how he'd always liked to brainstorm with pen and paper rather than being chained to his computer and a Word document.

She wrestled with her desire to walk out the door and not turn back. But in the end Mirror Glass Bay and her promise won out. She sat too.

He glanced across at her. He didn't smile, but she had to remind herself that the warmth in his eyes was not reflected in his heart. He'd given her no apology—not for then and not for now. Damon Macy took what he wanted, when he wanted, without apology. And without thought for how it might affect anyone else. She'd be a fool to forget it.

She sat, folded her arms and forced her spine to make contact with the back of the chair. She loathed Damon Macy and all he stood for, but she couldn't let her antipathy harm Mirror Glass Bay. If he really wanted to make amends, she intended to take full advantage of that. 'How will you fix it? Do you now plan to build that luxury resort?'

'I—' He broke off with a curse. 'I signed a non-compete clause. It was the only way I could get Greamsman to agree to the deal.'

Wow. His conscience must be making him feel really guilty. But then the meaning of his words hit her, and it was all she could do not to drop her head to her arms and cry. A non-compete clause meant Mirror Glass Bay could kiss goodbye to a luxury resort for good. The town needed an injection of capital. It needed development, jobs and infrastructure. Local government grants and initiatives were all given to Byron Bay, where the tourist dollar repaid it ten-fold. Mirror Glass Bay didn't aspire to those same standards. It just wanted a little piece of the pie—just enough to support a medical centre and to keep the tiny primary school open. It didn't seem too much to ask.

'Right.'

Damon straightened and the broad expanse of his shoulders squared, as if he were a superhero in a big-budget film getting ready for the fight of his life. It should've made her want to laugh in scorn and derision and call him unflattering names, such as *egotist* and *poseur*. No scorn or derision rose through her, though—at least, not any directed at him.

'I can build several state-of-the-art high-rises

on that site—luxury apartments.' He tapped the pen against his mouth. 'As long as I can get the necessary planning permissions.'

She dismissed that with a single wave of her hand. 'And who will live in them? Sure, their construction and outfitting will bring jobs to the area, but it's a short-term solution. Once they're done…'

'I could make them short-term holiday lets.'

'Besides the fact that brings you dangerously close to contravening your non-compete clause…'

'I'd make them family friendly, not luxury, and—'

'In which case you'd be stealing from my client base.'

He cursed again and went back to jotting notes on his pad. 'What about a theme park?'

'What about you do some proper research into the area first and find out the kinds of tourists Mirror Glass Bay—and Byron Bay, for that matter—attract? That is, if you're serious about helping.'

His gaze lifted, his eyes dark and intense. 'I'm serious.'

He'd always been too serious. Though she'd been able to make him laugh, had managed to get him to loosen up—back in the old days. Her hands clenched. Until he'd thrown her over for two million dollars to advance his goddamned career. He'd thrown away everything they'd had for…

She folded her arms. It didn't look as though it had brought him any joy.

Which served him right.

But it didn't seem fair that his hair should be as dark and glossy as it had always been, his jaw just as square and strong or his shoulders as broad and appealing. It wasn't fair that his outside should be so compelling, could make a woman's stomach soften with longing, when inside his heart was black.

He leaned back in his seat, his chin lifting. 'What's wrong with my theme park idea?'

'What am I now—your research assistant?'

Mirror Glass Bay needs help! If this man…

She dragged in a breath, moderated her tone. 'How far are we from the Gold Coast?'

'No idea. Three or four hours?'

'An hour and fifteen minutes.'

If he really wanted to make amends—if he was sincere—then his heart couldn't be that black, could it?

Her lips twisted. Maybe it was just a really dirty charcoal-grey.

'What?' he said, his hand lifting, as if to check his hair.

She snapped back to their conversation. 'How many theme parks are there on the Gold Coast?'

She watched him count them off on his fingers. He held up three and raised an eyebrow.

'Five,' she told him. 'So, if families or singles wanted a theme-park holiday, why would they come to Mirror Glass Bay when they could go to the Gold Coast?'

'Because my theme park would be the best.'

He still had that same old arrogance, the same belief he could make things happen, and it tugged at some secret, hidden place inside her. And for the first time since she'd clapped eyes on him again she was scared rather than shocked and angry. Scared that he still had the power to hurt her.

She set her shoulders and did what she could to get her thumping heart back under control. That'd only happen if she let it. And there was no way on God's green she was going to let it happen. *Ever.* She gripped her hands in her lap to counter their trembling. 'What is Byron Bay known for?'

'An amazing beach. An amazing *surfing* beach,' he clarified. 'The town has always attracted surfers and backpackers.' His lips pursed. 'It's also considered a hub of new age and hippy culture. From what I saw yesterday, very briefly, there are a lot of yoga retreats and holistic wellness centres in the area.'

'And do you think the kind of people who are attracted to those things—who come to this part of the world to experience those things—are the kind of people interested in rollercoasters and water slides?'

His pen started up a quick and annoying *tap-tap-tap* against his pad. She wanted to reach across and halt it, only that'd betray the calm composure she was trying to maintain.

'You're right,' he said slowly.

Hallelujah.

Except...

She frowned. 'About what?'

'I *do* need to research the area. Properly.' His eyes narrowed at whatever he saw in her face. 'I *am* going to fix this, Eve. You'll see.'

She hoped to God he did. Her community needed it. And as for herself... 'As long as you don't expect me to pin a medal on your chest at the end of all this, clap you on the shoulder and tell you what a great guy you are.'

Because he wasn't a great guy. And she had no intention of forgetting it.

'Don't worry, Evie,' he drawled. 'I'm keeping my fantasies firmly grounded in reality.'

She had to glance away at the word 'fantasies'. It conjured up too much, and she'd lost too much to him last time. 'Eve,' she corrected. 'Only my friends are allowed to call me Evie.' It'd taken her too long to pick herself up and find some joy in life again after the last time. That peace had become precious to her, and she wasn't letting him disturb it again.

'There's just one thing I want from you, *Eve*.'

To stay out of his hair?

She turned back and raised an eyebrow, crossing her fingers in her lap.

'I need a place to stay. I need you to find me a room in that motel of yours.'

No!

She didn't want this man anywhere near her beloved town. Mirror Glass Bay had become her haven and refuge. It'd saved her. It'd given her a new direction. It'd given her *hope*. If Damon Macy came crashing into her life now...

She halted that thought dead in its tracks. Mirror Glass Bay needed Damon to undo the damage he'd just done. And if she could hold him the least bit accountable then she owed it to her community.

She forced her lips upwards. 'You're in luck. It's off-season so you can have the Kingfisher Suite. It's our best.' Though he'd be used to much finer these days. 'And I'll charge you through the nose for it.'

His low laugh vibrated in all her hidden secret places. 'I wouldn't expect anything less.'

CHAPTER TWO

EVE DID HER best to assume nonchalance as she led Damon into her pride and joy—the Mirror Glass Bay Beachside Motel—and tried to see it objectively, as if through his eyes.

Tried and failed. The task was impossible. She'd thrown herself into this project four years ago after the scales had been lifted from her eyes—revealing the reality about both Damon and the corporate world upon which she'd pinned all her youthful dreams. The ruthlessness of the former and the savagery of the latter had shattered every ideal she'd ever had about becoming a self-made woman. To her so far never-ending relief, she'd discovered she wanted no part of either. She had no regrets about walking away.

She and her grandmother had jumped into Eve's snazzy little hatchback and had headed north before her parents could shove Gran into a retirement home and forget all about her. The two of them had washed up here in Mirror Glass Bay, eight-and-a-half hours north of Sydney. They'd taken one look at the rundown motel and had glimpsed the future they'd wanted to create.

From the corner of her eye she watched Damon take in every detail. She and Gran had pooled their resources, bought the motel and spent the last four years bringing it back to its former glory. That didn't change the fact that The Beachside, as it was affectionately known by the locals and its regulars, was nothing more than a three-star family motel.

A spick and span one.

A comfortable one.

A home-away-from-home one.

And a haven for Gran and her.

But a man like Damon wouldn't see any of that. Or, if he did, he wouldn't recognise its value. He'd simply see the lack of ostentation, the lack of five-star luxury, and that was his loss. She loved what she and Gran had achieved, and she refused to let the opinion of a man like Damon Macy belittle that achievement.

She nodded at her reception desk attendant. 'Bettina, this is Mr Damon Macy. He's going to be staying for…?' She turned to Damon and raised an eyebrow. 'For how long would you like to book the suite?'

One powerful shoulder lifted. 'What would you suggest?'

She'd like to suggest he take a hike so she

never had to see his handsome face again, but there was too much at stake. And she could be big enough to put Mirror Glass Bay's needs above her own pettiness. *Right?*

She comforted herself with the notion of unearthing whatever better nature he had and taking advantage of it—for the greater good of her community, of course—before his ruthless business sense kicked in and he walked away, dusting off his hands and the challenge Mirror Glass Bay presented.

She kept her expectations within the realms of the possible, though. 'Shall we start with a three-night stay, then?' That would give the town committee the shadow of a chance to showcase the area to its best advantage. He'd at least get a taste for what the place had to offer.

'Do you really think three nights is long enough for me to get a proper grasp of the unique issues Mirror Glass Bay faces?' he drawled, one eyebrow raised sardonically in enquiry, as if he could see through her mask of calm business composure and was mocking her for her lack of ambition—for not demanding more of him.

But she'd demanded more from him once before and he'd failed her. She had no faith left now.

'Absolutely not. A fortnight might do it justice. But I was keeping my expectations...*realistic.*'

She smiled—oh, she made sure she smiled—but her words were laced with a poison that had Bettina's eyes widening.

She doubted Damon noticed, or cared about, Bettina's reaction. He angled his chin towards Eve and placed those long-fingered hands on his hips. 'Let your fantasies go wild, Eve. Ask for what you want. Who knows? You might even get it.'

She recalled a time when she'd have slipped her arms about his waist, tucked her head against his shoulder and relished all of that warm male strength. Her mouth dried and it took all her strength not to take a step away from him. His gaze lowered and she knew he could see the pulse in her throat hammering.

She hated that. Hated that she couldn't control her reaction. Hated that her body betrayed her. Hated that he knew it—*that* was what she hated most of all. She refused to let her chin drop. So what if he knew she wasn't as calm as she pretended to be? The one thing he couldn't be certain of was why.

And she had no intention of admitting that she found him every bit as thrilling and potently attractive as ever.

She swung back to Bettina. 'Book Mr Macy into the Kingfisher Suite for two weeks.'

He wouldn't stay for two weeks.

He handed his credit card over without a murmur.

She sent him a big, fake smile. 'You'll be pleased to know that we're currently running a deal—stay five nights and get the sixth night free.'

'Absolutely delighted,' he returned, slotting his credit card back into its folder and slipping it into the inside pocket of his suit jacket. 'How...'

If he said *quaint* she might just have to hit him.

'Fortuitous. Some might even say auspicious.'

Smart man.

'Our usual clientele appreciates the chance to stay with us for as long as possible. We like to facilitate that whenever we can.'

'Very generous of you.'

She ignored his sarcasm and took the key from Bettina. 'We're a modest establishment but pride ourselves on our hospitality.' Another big, fake smile. 'We don't have any porters here, Damon, but I'm more than happy to carry your bag for you if you require it.'

He snapped back from his comprehensive perusal of the small motel reception to seize his bag. 'I'm happy to carry my own bag, thank you.' He gestured to the doors—one led left, one led right and there was the one behind them that led back to the street where they'd parked their cars. 'Lead the way.'

She took him through the left door and back

outside, where she promptly ascended a set of stairs. 'This is the oldest part of the complex. It used to be a seaman's mission but was decommissioned fifty years ago and turned into a motel.'

When they reached the first floor, with its deep veranda that ran the length of the building, she gestured at the beach spread out before them. 'This is why people pay a few extra dollars a night for the rooms in this part of the motel.'

Because the beach was beautiful.

To their left a residential road perpendicular to the one they'd parked on ran parallel to the beach. To their right was nothing but sand dunes, beach and the headland. 'We parked our cars on Beach Road, and that one—' she gestured to the road that ran beside the beach '—is called Marine Drive. Both roads will bring you back to the motel.'

He didn't answer and she turned to find he'd stopped dead, his mouth agape. 'This is…'

'Rather pretty,' she agreed, deliberately minimising the impact of the view and setting a brisk pace along the wooden floorboards to the door at its very end.

'*Rather* pretty?' he spluttered as she unlocked his door.

She turned to survey the view again, moving to stand by the veranda railing, because it was easier than looking at him. How she loved this place. It fed her soul in ways she needed. She didn't want to imagine life away from here.

And she didn't have to, she told herself.

'You can see why our guests will snap up that extra night for free if they can.'

He'd dropped his bag and joined her at the railing. 'I—'

'But it lacks the grandeur of the main beach at Byron Bay. Or the views of Sydney Harbour from the Toaster,' she added, referring to an iconic luxury apartment complex on Circular Quay—which was probably where he lived these days.

'It has its own charm.'

He smelled of boardrooms—of printer ink, mints and air conditioning—but beneath it was a hint of spice that had her nose wrinkling in appreciation. 'On a good day the surf here can't be beaten, but it can also be uneven and...pernickety. Dedicated surfers prefer Byron. The headland, though, means it's a safe swimming beach. Young families love it.'

She couldn't have said why but the arrested expression on his face satisfied her.

She pointed away from the nearby headland and down Marine Drive. 'Can you see the scrub at the far end of the road?'

'Yes.'

'That's what you just bought from Mr Greamsman. Beachfront land that abuts national park, which means the site is loaded with both charm… and potential.'

She didn't glance up into his face. She didn't want to see his expression. She had little belief, despite his protestations otherwise, that he would see any project there through. She'd do her best to convince him otherwise—she had to do at least that much. What was it Gran always said? *Where there's life, there's hope.* But she didn't believe Damon would deliver on his promise.

'And this is your room.' She swung away from the glorious view to open his door and motioned for him to precede her. For a moment she thought he might refuse, but then he seemed to recall his status as guest and hers as motel manager, and he strode through the doorway, lips pressed together in a thin line. She meant to make sure he didn't forget that distinction. She meant to preserve the boundary—all the boundaries: guest and worker, small businesswoman and wealthy developer, concerned citizen and potential saviour. Because that was all that mattered here. The fact that they had once been lovers was of no consequence.

Yeah, right. Tell yourself that enough, sunshine, and you might just start to believe it.

Not wanting to look into his face again—not wanting to see the dismissiveness she fully expected to see in his eyes as he inspected his accommodation—she motioned towards the coffee table with its small array of brochures. 'We do what it says in the fine print—provide comfortable accommodation. This is the bedroom.' She opened a door to the left and moved in to open the French doors leading back out to the veranda and those beach views.

When she turned, he was there, staring at her. She knew he wasn't thinking of her as motel worker or small businesswoman, but she refused to let her gaze, her attention or her fantasies dwell on the enormous king-sized bed. Instead she sailed back past him into the main living area where she swept the curtains aside to reveal a glass sliding door at the rear of the room that led out to a balcony. Opening the door, she let in a fresh breeze that swept through from the front doorway—a breeze scented with salt and sun. She closed her eyes and drew it into her lungs.

She felt him move towards her and she opened her eyes and lifted her chin. 'You'll get a better idea of the layout of the complex from out here.'

'The motel is more than the converted seaman's mission?'

She moved outside before he could reach her, letting the warm autumn air move across her skin. She gave what she really, *really* hoped was an expansive gesture. 'As you can now see for yourself.'

There was room for a small café-style table and chairs out here on the balcony, but he ignored them to rest his forearms against the wrought-iron railing and gaze out across at her complex.

'We parked on the road, but feel free to drive your hire car in and park it beneath one of the carports.' She gestured to where there was parking for a dozen cars. 'There's overflow parking on the next block, but as it's not high season it's not in use at the moment.'

The driveway was located on the other side of Reception. She pointed. 'There's a one-bedroom flat above Reception, which is where I live.' On the other side of the driveway a white stucco building stretched away from them, facing the road, and she gestured to that next. 'That's the family accommodation over there.'

'So this is...?' He tapped the railing to indicate the building they were in.

'More for couples and singles. The family accommodation is more budget-friendly, and has easy access to the pool and lawn area where children can play.' She gestured to the large green quadrangle in front of them with an in-ground pool at its centre. 'There are picnic tables down there, showers and a barbecue station.'

Palm trees dotted the area along with an enormous jacaranda, the fronds and branches waving happily in the breeze. Hibiscus bushes in flower added splashes of colour. Damon shook his head. 'This is…'

She told herself she didn't care what he thought, but rather than interrupt him she found herself holding her breath.

'Really nice,' he finished.

She might've taken offence at such an insipid word if he hadn't loaded it with so much wonder.

She shrugged. 'It's home.'

He straightened, rising to his full height, but she kept her gaze trained on the grounds below. 'The bottom floor of the north wing—' she gestured to the white building '—houses the restaurant-cum-breakfast room, cum-café and bar.' It was one of the few meeting places Mirror Glass Bay could boast, and the local residents took full advantage of it.

He gestured to the building directly opposite. 'Is that part of the complex too?'

She didn't blame him for asking. It was in another style entirely—three storeys of plain blond brick. 'Those are the longer-let apartments.' Her grandmother lived in one of the ground-floor ones and she made a mental note to keep her away from Damon.

'So…you cater to different styles of clientele?'

'Within reason. And there is some overlap.'

'How many rooms all up?'

'Sixteen here in The Mission. These are our premier rooms—large, generous, olde worlde.'

'And all boasting that amazing view.'

The view was key.

'We have thirty-two rooms of various sizes and configurations in the north wing. And there are a dozen apartments in that west wing. Some of those, though, are let to permanent residents.'

'Why did you choose this room for me?'

'Because it's the best.' She shrugged. 'And because of the view.' If she'd thought for a moment he'd stay for a fortnight, she'd have considered an apartment for him.

But she hadn't. And he wouldn't. So it was a moot point.

'So you have a beachside wing, a north wing and a west wing.'

'Which are, of course, terribly unimaginative names. This—' she tapped the balcony railing '—is affectionately referred to as The Mission. That—' she pointed to the white stucco building '—is the Shangri La. While the apartment block is called The Nest.'

He gestured to the south. 'And that?'

'Is a nature reserve and can't be built on.'

This odd jumble of buildings shouldn't work but it did. It held all the charm of a bygone era and he found himself responding to its warmth and promise.

She'd called it home. It felt like how home should feel.

He had an apartment on Sydney Harbour—not in the Toaster, but down on the waterfront. He had his own private jetty, but he didn't have a boat. The views were incredible, but he couldn't remember the last time he'd stepped out onto his jetty. It was considered one of the most enviable locations in the country, yet he had a growing suspicion that he didn't love it the way Eve loved her little one-bedroom flat above Reception.

He had everything a man could want—wealth, power, position—yet…

Yet none of it could plug the hole inside him.

The only time he'd ever felt whole was when he'd been with Eve. And he'd sacrificed that.

He glanced at her now. She'd grown her hair and it'd lightened almost to blonde in places. The colour could've come from a bottle…or from how much time she spent in the sun. He suspected the latter, considering the way she wore barely any make-up.

He remembered watching her in the mornings as she'd applied a full face of make-up. He'd always told her she didn't need any of it, that she was beautiful without it. She'd told him it was her uniform. At the time, the thought that he was the only one to see her as she truly was—her unmade self—had dazzled him.

Now it appeared she let everyone see her as she was, and he sensed she was the happier for it; happier in her own skin.

He let no one see him as he really was. The thought had him dragging a hand down his face.

'You look tired. I'll leave you to rest.'

'No!' The word fired out of him too fast and with too much force, taking him as much off-guard as it did her. She raised an eyebrow and his collar tightened about his throat. 'Have dinner with me tonight?'

The request slipped from him—soft and almost begging—and he held his breath.

Surprise flickered across her face, and what looked suspiciously like confusion, before she abruptly turned away to stride back into the living room with its big comfy-looking sofas at right angles to each other, its table for two and large antique desk. She'd made the room feel more welcoming than an entire team of designers had his Sydney apartment.

'I'm sorry, Damon, I have plans tonight.'

Though her tone told him that her answer would've been a blunt no even if she hadn't had plans.

Two things struck him at the same time then. She might've changed her hair, and she mightn't bother with make-up and business suits any more, but her shoulders still went tight when she was angry. And her eyes still held that same remote expression they always had whenever she held her anger in check. She wanted to tell him to go to hell, but something held her back. This development must mean a lot to her.

He swallowed. He'd promised to fix things. That didn't come with conditions. He'd fix this, somehow, whether she was pleasant to him or not. And that was what he should be turning his mind to— making amends, not having dinner with a woman who had no desire to dine with him or to revisit the past.

The second thing that hit him was, was she seeing someone? It was none of his business. *None.* Once in his head, though, the thought refused to let him go. His hands clenched. It was likely, though, wasn't it? At thirty-two, she was still young. And more beautiful than she'd ever been. Somewhere at the centre of his being a howl started up.

What the hell...?

'That wasn't meant to sound like a romantic overture.'

Liar.

'I just want to know more about Mirror Glass Bay, and you're in a position to tell me everything I need to know.'

'The answer is still *I'm busy.*'

Her shoulders remained tight and her eyes remote.

'We don't do room service at The Beachside, but you have tea-and coffee-making facilities in your room. And, as I mentioned before, there's a café-cum-restaurant and bar on the ground floor of the Shangri La. Breakfast, lunch and dinner are all served there. In addition to that, there's a block of shops on Marine Drive including a tiny supermarket, a takeaway, and a café. Remember—Marine Drive runs parallel to the beach, Beach Road runs perpendicular.'

She repeated her earlier directions as if unaware she'd had his full attention from the moment she'd stepped into that boardroom in Byron several hours ago.

She glanced at his business suit and shoes, and he could almost read the 'not suitable beachside attire' in her eyes, but she said nothing.

'I suggest you take your time to familiarise yourself with the town and what it has to offer the potential developer. Most afternoons, I can be found in Reception or the bar.'

It wasn't exactly an invitation, but he clutched the scrap like a lifeline.

'I hope your stay will be very pleasant.'

Then she was gone, and he found himself blinking in the sudden silence. He throbbed all over, as if he'd been hit by a bus, but that made no sense whatsoever.

He shook himself. What the hell was he doing? He needed to ring Owen…and the office. He needed to find out all he could about the environmental injunction on Greamsman's proposed development, pore over the development-control plan and find out all he could about Mirror Glass Bay pronto.

He was a man who made things happen. He had to find a solution and get the hell out of town ASAP because it was clear Eve didn't want to re-visit their shared past. He had no right raking it all up and disturbing her peace.

He knew how much he'd hurt her.

Because he'd hurt himself too—just as much.

You didn't get over that kind of hurt overnight. But Eve had rebuilt her life. She'd moved on. He had no right dragging her back and causing her further havoc. He'd come here to help, not hurt her again.

He'd do everything he could to make sure that didn't happen. Even if everything inside him hungered for a second chance with the only woman he'd ever loved.

Not going to happen.

And the sooner he got over it the better. For everyone.

Pulling out his phone, he started to punch in Owen's number, but caught a glimpse of ocean from his open door and paused mid-dial. That doorway full of sea and sun, the way the light danced and dazzled, had him pulling in a lung-ful of clean air.

It'd be the middle of the night in Europe. Not that consideration for time zones had stopped him in the past, but... The sun danced on the

sea, glinting gold on the sand, and the breeze
had everything pulsing with life and play. He
pushed his phone back into his pocket and instead strode into his bedroom to retrieve his
laptop.

The view from his bedroom's French doors
was even better, and he kicked off his shoes,
settled on the bed with four big pillows propped
at his back and started to compose an email to
his VP. *My plans have changed. Not coming to
Frankfurt. Apologise to Herr Mueller and return
to Australia on the next available flight.*

He went to hit Send but froze. He was being
watched. Very slowly he raised his eyes to find
a tabby cat standing in a patch of sun just outside the French doors, staring at him with tawny
eyes.

Where on earth had it come from?

He blinked. It blinked.

He pulled in a breath and straightened.

It sat, its tail curling around itself in a neat
circle.

Should he shoo it away? Ignore it? Was it Eve's
cat? The thought made his heart beat harder.
Maybe she had a boyfriend *and* a cat.

He rubbed the spot above his left eyebrow.
'Well, puss, while you're not wearing a collar,
you look too well-fed to be a stray.'

As if his words were the encouragement it
had been looking for, the cat bounded into his

room like a dog and jumped up onto his bed with a meow.

What the…?

Before he thought better of it, he reached out and stroked a finger beneath the cat's jaw. A loud rumble of approval greeted him. 'I thought you cats were supposed to be aloof and grumpy.'

The tabby curled against Damon's thigh, its head bumping his hand for more attention. He chuckled. 'I've met your kind before—a con artist, a confidence trickster.'

He stroked the purring cat for several moments and then glanced back at his laptop. 'What am I going to do about Owen, puss? He's put an awful lot of work into the Mueller project.' He bit back a sigh. 'The thing is, though, Mueller isn't the kind of man who agrees to work with an underling.' Still, few people would consider the VP of Macy Holdings an underling.

He stared out at all that dancing blue sea. 'I could give him the go-ahead—tell him to give it his best shot if he wants to, I guess. If he thinks it's a lost cause, he can come home. But if he wants to try…?'

The cat's purr sounded throughout the room as Damon's fingers threaded through the soft fur. It wouldn't hurt to let Owen at least try. With a nod, he sent an email telling Owen to follow his instincts.

Next he rang his PA and told him to reschedule his meetings for the next three weeks, to pass them off to some of the senior executives.

His fingers hovered over the keyboard. He should get a comprehensive report on Mirror Glass Bay, but he couldn't stop his gaze from drifting back to the view of the beach. He closed his laptop with a decisive click. He could research that kind of stuff online tonight when he had nothing better to do except wonder what Eve's *plans* were.

He glanced at his suitcase. He'd packed suits and workout clothes. That was it. With a sigh he changed into tracksuit bottoms, a long-sleeved T-shirt and his trainers.

He paused at the sight of the cat curled up in the middle of the bed. 'I'm going out now, puss.'

It didn't move and he didn't have the heart to disturb it. This was probably the kind of place where people didn't need to lock their doors. He could probably leave one of the French doors open… He glanced at his laptop and shook his head. He couldn't risk it. Instead he left a saucer of water for the cat in case it got thirsty and let himself out of the door, locking it behind him.

A breeze ruffled his hair, its warmth taking him off-guard and reminding him he was eight hours north of Sydney—close to the border of tropical Queensland. In Sydney, people would be wrapping up as autumn took hold. But here he could wear short sleeves—if he had them.

Maybe he'd get lucky and discover that Mirror Glass Bay boasted a clothing shop. Regardless, it was time to go and explore.

It took him four and a half minutes to reach the shops. The supermarket was also a post office and boasted a huge range of ice-creams. There were caps and a couple of souvenir T-shirts, but that was it as far as clothing went. There was also a surf shop that looked like it sold swimwear—including designer board shorts and T-shirts. Except it was only open at the weekend. Ditto with the takeaway. And as it was only Tuesday…

A café sprawled on the corner of the next block. The concertina windows, all pushed wide open, flooded the place with light. He took a seat at the counter that ran the window's length and stared out at the beach.

Mirror Glass Bay was amazing…beautiful. He stared and stared. It was every boyhood dream he'd ever had about the beach and what he'd do with his life if he could ever get away from the dingy inner-city slum where he'd grown up. But, while the town might be a boyhood dream, there was nothing here other than the beach.

Were there any schools? What about doctors or a clinic? Did the town boast a sporting team of any kind? Who lived here—retirees? Singles and young couples? Families?

He pulled out his phone…no service. He shook it, but that didn't make a scrap of difference.

'We're in a black spot here, love,' a waitress said, bustling up. 'A block in either direction, and you can pick up service again, but here...' She trailed off, her shrug eloquent. 'What can I get for you?'

He glanced at the specials board. 'What would you recommend?'

'The fish tacos are particularly good,' she said without hesitation.

He ordered the fish tacos, and was about to add a long black coffee to his order, but glanced out at the beach, changed his mind and requested a glass of iced tea instead.

To his surprise, the place filled up around him. Where had all these people come from?

'Have you heard? Word's out that the resort has fallen through.'

His ears pricked up.

'Nah, mate, it'll be those darn environmentalists up to their old tricks again. What's the bet?'

'What—like them stupid sods who tried to stop that development on the other side of Byron for some rare orchid that had supposedly been found?' a third voice asked.

'Yeah, but turns out they'd planted it themselves to try and scare the developer off.'

'Fingers crossed our guy has more gumption than that.'

'So far all you've got is an unconfirmed rumour, Ron Seymour,' the waitress said, cutting through their chatter. 'I'll thank you not to go starting a panic just yet.'

'Evie Clark'll know,' someone said.

'We can ask her at the meeting tonight.'

A meeting?

Damon swung round on his stool to face the table behind. 'Excuse me, I couldn't help but overhear your conversation. Please allow me to introduce myself...'

CHAPTER THREE

EVE GLANCED UP from her phone and Beck's text message to watch yet another noisy group of Mirror Glass Bay residents stride into the school hall—the school they all desperately wanted to keep. She'd known there'd be more people than usual here tonight, but they'd exceeded her expectations. They'd had to set out more chairs. Twice. At this rate it would be standing room only soon.

Which suited her just fine, as koala conservation was a topic close to her heart. And that was what tonight's meeting was *officially* about. The town might be hopping with rumours, but she was going to make sure they stuck to the order of business first. General town gossip could take place afterwards over a cup of tea and a biscuit.

She glanced at the urn. They didn't have enough biscuits.

Huffing out a laugh, she shook her head. Biscuits didn't matter.

Her phone vibrated. She read the text and then stood and clapped her hands. 'Okay, everyone, Beck is running a bit late, so she's ordered me to start the meeting without her.' Beck Daniels was president of the Mirror Glass Bay Koala Conservation Group and also Parks and Wildlife's resident scientist. Eve was the group's treasurer.

'I'll leave it to her to update us on all of the most recent sightings, findings and numbers. The big thing on the agenda this month is the working bee we need to organise. The southern and western boundaries of the koala sanctuary are being encroached upon by a variety of non-native plants. If they go unchecked, they'll run rampant through the reserve and overtake...'

She stopped dead when Damon sauntered into the hall with Ron Seymour and his team of carpenters.

What on earth...?

Damon had ditched the suit for a pair of cotton twill work shorts, a high-vis shirt and work boots. She swallowed and glanced away. She preferred a man in a suit.

She glanced back. *Liar.*

Thankfully the entire room had turned to stare or she might've become an object of rumour herself. She wiped damp palms down the front of her jeans.

Damon and his new friends took seats at the

back of the hall and all heads swung back to her. What the heck? She might as well use the town's curiosity to her advantage.

Pulling in a breath, she pasted on a smile. 'I suspect most of you will have heard that we have a new developer in town. I will introduce Mr Macy just as soon as we've got through tonight's order of business. So...' she picked up her clipboard '...we need volunteers for the working bee this Saturday.'

So far they only had half a dozen names on the list. A few additional people raised their hands. She jotted the names down, biting back a sigh. 'A good turnout means we'll be done by lunch time. To sweeten the deal, The Beachside will be holding a sausage sizzle afterwards for all of the helpers.'

Damon immediately raised his hand. She tried to stop her eyebrows from shooting up. Did he know what he was volunteering for? Weeding a marshy scrub was mucky work. A murmur went around the room and slowly more hands were raised.

Beck, who'd been standing at the side door, came striding in now. She pointed a finger at the collective crowd. 'I know each and every one of you. If you don't show on Saturday, I'll be demanding an explanation.'

But she said it with a smile and a ripple of laughter went around the hall.

Eve sat as Beck gave her regular report on the small koala population. Thirty koalas currently resided in the Mirror Glass Bay sanctuary. She detailed reported sightings and warned motorists to drive slowly on the strip of road between Cockatoo Avenue and Dolphin Street, as it was the corridor some koalas were taking between pockets of swamp eucalyptus that was their only food source.

'And finally,' she said, 'our treasurer warns me that funds are running low. Our local veterinarians go above and beyond in providing their time and services free of charge, but the conservation group has to cover the costs of all medicines and equipment used. I'd appreciate it if everyone could start thinking about ways we could raise funds. We'll continue applying for whatever grants we can, but every dollar counts, and it'd be an enormous ecological loss if this koala population was to dwindle further. We'll discuss that at our next meeting.'

While Eve heard Beck's words, and agreed with them wholeheartedly, all her attention was focused on the back of the room. Her eyes resolutely looked forward, but she could feel Damon's physical presence in the room. Which was crazy. She told herself it was just her mind playing tricks. But the image of him in that work gear... Her mouth dried. He looked so capable, so competent, so...*hot*.

Stop it.

This had nothing to do with what he looked like. What he looked like should have no bearing on *anything*. Prince or troll, all that mattered was that he held the fate of the town in his hands.

'Thank you, everyone, for your interest. It's heartening to see so many people here.'

Beck's wryness had a smile tugging at Eve's lips. A glance at her watch confirmed it was the quickest meeting ever.

'Does that mean the meeting is officially over?' Ron called from the back.

'It does,' Beck confirmed with a nod.

Ron shot to his feet. 'Then I'd like to introduce Damon Macy to everyone who managed to get here tonight. Come on, mate.'

Eve, who'd started to rise to make the promised introduction, subsided back into her seat as Ron and Damon made their way to the front of the hall.

'Damon here has taken over the development site from that other guy, who for reasons of his own has done a bunk and hightailed it out of here. For legal reasons, Damon can't build a resort on that land, so what he wants from the folks here tonight are some ideas for what we'd like to see developed on that site.'

'A hospital...a modern medical centre...a retirement village!' someone shouted out.

'Shops,' a group of teenagers chimed in. 'Dress shops! Shoe shops! Jewellery shops!

'A business centre.'

'A function centre.'

The suggestions came thick and fast and Damon raised his hands for quiet as everyone started to speak at once. He looked totally at ease in his work gear, which shouldn't have surprised her. He'd never had any trouble commanding the attention of a boardroom. But he must have lackeys to do this kind of on-the-ground reconnaissance for him these days.

Still, it couldn't be denied that when he raised his hands everyone quietened down and waited. Unexpectedly he grinned, and as his gaze roved about the room she was sure that more than one female heart fluttered.

Not hers, though. Oh, no, not hers. She folded her arms and willed steel to her spine.

'First of all, I want to say how pleased I am to meet you all.'

He sounded as if he meant every word.

He's a liar. Don't forget he's a liar.

'I'm impressed already at the number of ideas that have been thrown into the ring. I wish my PR people could be as quick on the uptake with ideas as you have all been.'

Yeah, well, evidently his PR people weren't as motivated as the people in this room. Their town was in danger of becoming a ghost town—

a place without amenities. Her stomach screwed up tight.

'But I'm feeling a tad guilty about hijacking the Koala Conservation Group's meeting. So how about we brainstorm a few fundraising ideas for them first?'

She blinked. She couldn't think of a single darn thing to say. Which was fine, as nothing was expected of her, but...

He smiled down at her, his mouth lifting into an amused curve, as if he was fully aware of her confusion. 'So here's an idea I've had off the top of my head—how about an auction? This town has a lot to offer, right?'

Of course, it did. Suggesting otherwise would get him lynched.

A variety of yeses sounded around the room.

'How about auctioning off a variety of services and goods that the people of Mirror Glass Bay can provide to showcase the town's talent and—?'

'Who to?' someone shouted out. 'Who would come other than other Mirror Glass Bay folk? We already know what's on offer in town, so what's the point?'

'Pull your head in, Jeff,' Ron said.

'No, it's a fair criticism.' Damon tapped a finger against his lips as he strode up and down the front of the room. Everyone held their breath as they watched. Even Eve.

We're all fools, she told herself.

'I can get my PR people to spread the word, but we need something to tempt those from further afield.' He straightened. 'We could make a night of it. We could have a dance. I'll organise a headline band to draw the crowd in if Eve Clark will agree to donate the bar and restaurant at The Beachside as the venue.'

'Absolutely,' she agreed without hesitation.

People started shouting out things they'd donate for the auction—handmade candles and soaps, a pest inspection from the pest controllers. The freelance bookkeeper offered a free tax return…the local seamstress offered garment-mending and alterations.

'We might need your clipboard,' Damon said with a smile to Eve and Beck.

Beck handed the clipboard to Eve. 'You better take the lead on this.'

'Why?' The other woman rarely took a back seat. Beck was a doer. She loved being in the thick of things.

'I'll explain later.'

There was no time to probe her further. Eve joined Damon and Ron on the floor, jotting down the services and products offered. The variety was wonderful—from babysitting to professional photographs, house cleaning to barbecue cleaning, and from free computer training to free websites. Eve offered up a two-night stay at The Beachside.

She read the list out loud, shaking her head when she reached the end. 'This is amazing.' She glanced at Damon. 'It was a nice idea.'

A nice idea? It was a *great* idea.

He shrugged. 'Only because the entire town has got behind it.'

She glanced around the room, because it was far less confronting and much less confusing than looking at Damon. Why was he doing this? Why was he taking such an interest in Mirror Glass Bay and its doings?

The answer came swiftly. Money, of course. He'd want his investment here to make him money. The far from romantic reality of financial returns had her straightening and the fog in her mind lifting. For as long as he was here, they could take advantage of it. The Koala Conservation Group needed every penny it could get.

As if he sensed her scepticism, he turned to her and one side of his mouth hooked up. 'Do we want to set a date for our auction?'

Beck nodded and mouthed an exaggeratedly urgent, *'Yes.'*

Eve had to fight the sudden urge to hit Damon over the head with her clipboard. Her frustration made no sense—he was doing good, albeit for reasons of his own.

She swallowed. The frustration came from the past she'd thought she'd left behind four long years ago.

He can't hurt you any more.

That was true. But his lack of interest could hurt Mirror Glass Bay.

She moistened her lips, her senses sharpening. The Damon she'd once known had never been able to resist a challenge. She lifted her chin and stuck out a hip. 'How long do you need to find a suitable band and book them in?'

A spark fired to life in the back of his eyes at her thinly veiled challenge. 'I can move fast. I'm a man who makes things happen.'

'Oh, really?' She folded her arms, pressing the clipboard to her chest. 'Then how does six weeks this Saturday sound?'

It sounded impossible to her. He'd be gone before this current week was out. And there was no way he'd still be here in six weeks.

We don't need him. We just need his band.

'Done.'

He had to be joking! She lifted her chin even higher. 'If you can get a quality band in that time, then that sounds perfect to me. What does everybody else think?'

Shouts of assent sounded all around them and the date was locked in.

Damon's smile encompassed the entire room. 'I see this is a town that makes things happen.

I'm proud I get to work with people who are so committed. Right.' He clapped his hands. 'Now that I've allayed my guilt about hijacking the meeting, we can return to some development ideas. I like what you've come up with so far, and I'll definitely be looking into several of those ideas, but I'd like to hear more.'

More ideas were touted—from manufacturing and boat-building to a yoga retreat and day spa.

'What about a research facility?' Beck finally said. 'One that could run educational programmes on the local wildlife, review dune rehabilitation…consider ways to protect and enhance the koala population?'

'Nice try, Beck.' Eve shook her head. 'Damon's an investor, not a philanthropist.'

Beck stood, her eyes turning serious and her mouth growing grim. 'I'm sorry, folks, but I need to throw a proverbial spanner in the works. Before I say anything more, just remember I'm the messenger here, not the decision maker.'

She looked as if she were facing a firing squad. Eve touched her friend's elbow. 'Beck?'

'I'm speaking now as employee of National Parks and Wildlife. An environmental protection order has been placed on Damon's development site. Evidence has emerged that it could be the nesting ground of the white-bellied storm petrel—a vulnerable species. I'm sorry, everyone, but until further investigation takes place all development will be stalled.'

Eve swung to Damon and the expression on his face had her sucking in a breath. He'd known!

But…it made no sense. 'That's the reason Greamsman walked away?' The question burst from her, but she didn't care.

He nodded.

But then that meant… 'Why didn't you mention it earlier?' He'd inherited *a mess*.

'Because I didn't have all the facts. I still don't.' He squared his shoulders and met her gaze. 'I promised I'd make this right, Eve. And I'm going to keep that promise.'

She knew then that the money meant nothing to him.

That was the precise moment Eve finally believed him. It was also the first time she looked at him properly, as if she really saw him. She looked him full in the face with those clear green eyes, her gaze not veering from his, and his world tilted.

It didn't just tilt but went whirling off its axis.

He wanted to swear, and swear some more, as the meeting finished up and dissolved around him. People carried the chairs to the back of the room and stacked them in neat rows. He helped and said goodbye to people as they called goodbye to him. But all the while his mind raced.

When he'd betrayed Eve four years ago, he'd

broken his own heart. He'd known that was what he was doing at the time, but it hadn't stopped him from choosing his career over her.

If he stayed here, he'd be in danger of breaking his heart again.

His mouth dried and his heart pumped so hard he could barely draw breath. His immediate instinct was to flee. To get the hell out of Dodge before he managed to annihilate all of his hard-won peace of mind.

Peace of mind?

Ha! He didn't have any of that. He didn't deserve any of that. But he'd learned to live with what he'd done. To open that wound again...

His hands clenched. If he could make things right now, though...? Maybe then he'd earn a measure of peace. He craved that—a sense of redemption—it was an ache in his soul.

Eve and Beck continued to talk, their heads close together. He put Beck at around fifty, but she'd seemed to age twenty years when she'd told the assembled meeting about the environmental protection order. The fate of the town mattered to her as much as it did to everyone else who'd attended tonight. Eve said something that made Beck laugh and lifted some of the weight from the older woman's shoulders.

He swore again—softly, under his breath. Eve had always done that. She'd always been focused on her work. She'd always been fiercely clever, ridiculously quick, and yet she'd been shockingly kind. She'd always taken the time to make her colleagues feel good about themselves, had done what she could to help reduce everyone's stress levels. At Spellman and Spelman's her team had been the happiest.

He couldn't get the hell out of Dodge—and it had nothing to do with earning some peace. He'd promised to help fix this problem—he'd promised to help her town. She hadn't asked him to—hadn't demanded it of him. But he'd made that promise just the same. And he wasn't breaking another promise to Eve. He wasn't breaking a promise to a woman who had never broken hers.

Eve and Beck hugged, and then Eve strode towards him. He wasn't a hundred per cent sure why, but he found himself straightening.

'Are you heading back to The Beachside?' she asked.

He nodded.

'Then we might as well keep each other company.'

He fell into step beside her as they walked the two blocks back to the motel. She didn't speak, so he remained silent too.

'Did you want a drink?' she asked abruptly, just as he thought she'd head inside to the bright lights of the bar and bid him goodnight.

'Sure.'

'Scotch?'

She remembered? 'Please.'

She led him up to the bar. 'Hey, Cass, this is Damon Macy. Damon, this is Cassidy Evans, my bar and restaurant manager, right-hand woman and best friend.'

'Pleased to meet you,' he said.

Cassidy was a tall, bronzed brunette—utterly gorgeous—and his stomach clenched at the look she sent him. She didn't return his greeting, just gave a curt nod in his general direction.

She knew.

She knew about his and Eve's history. Acid coated his tongue.

'Two Scotches, please, Cassidy. The good stuff.'

'I'll make them doubles, shall I?' She nodded down the other end of the bar where a group sat nursing beers. 'I heard about the meeting.'

'Good news travels fast,' he said.

The brunette shot him a glare that should've shrivelled him. 'As does the bad.'

He didn't need to be a rocket scientist to know which category she filed him under.

Eve took their tumblers and led the way to a small table at the far end of the room that had a view of the street outside. He couldn't see the beach from here, but he could hear it and smell it from the open windows.

'Cold?' Eve asked.

He shook his head. 'It's mild here compared

to Sydney.' He sipped his Scotch. 'Your friend Cassidy knows about our past.' He didn't mean the words to sound accusatory, and they weren't. At least, he didn't think they were, but they held an edge he wished he could temper.

'There are two people here who know our history. Cassidy is one and my grandmother is the other. Neither are going to be big fans of yours.' She sent him one of those piercing glances that had always cut through the nonsense and got to the heart of a matter. 'And if that bugs you then you should take more care not to do things that make you ashamed of yourself.'

He didn't answer that. What was there to say? She had no idea how much he regretted— *hated*—what he'd done. But, even if she did, it wasn't her job to ease his guilt and make him feel better.

'Sorry.' She glanced away. 'That was uncalled for.'

Hell, now she was feeling guilty!

He opened his mouth to tell her to forget it, but a couple of late diners left, shouting out a farewell to Eve before they exited into the night. Eve smiled and waved, and the moment was lost.

He watched them go and then turned back to her, a frown growing. 'Everyone knows you. In four years, you've become part of the fabric of this town—necessary, vital…' *Loved.* 'How'd you do that? I thought it took something like twenty years before you started being considered a local in a small town like this.'

Her lips pulled up into a genuine grin, rather than one of the practised smiles she'd so far reserved for him. It made his heart quicken. 'My grandmother grew up here. She moved when she married, but she brought me here for summer holidays when I was little. So I was practically a local before I bought The Beachside.'

She sipped her drink and then gestured at him. 'Where'd you get the gear?'

It was his turn to smile. He'd become so accustomed to suits, he'd forgotten how good it felt to get around in casual clothes. He told her about meeting Ron and his crew at the café, and how they'd taken him to the industrial site on the outskirts of town, from where he'd been able to buy work clothes from the factory outlet. In return for their time, he'd helped out with their current kitchen renovation job.

She stared at him. 'You spent the afternoon helping fit out Elsie Hitchcock's kitchen?'

The afternoon had been surprisingly enjoyable. 'I need to learn what issues are affecting the town. And Ron and his crew seemed as good a place to start as any. They certainly didn't pull their punches.'

Just for a moment, her eyes danced. 'Ron also wouldn't have minded showcasing his team's carpentry skills to the guy who's just bought the Greamsman site.'

'I told him off the bat what the deal was.' He hadn't wanted to take advantage of the other men.

'He'd have appreciated that. Which is why he dragged you to the meeting tonight.'

'And got word out to all and sundry to turn up if they could.'

She pursed her lips, her brow furrowing. 'I didn't know you had building skills.'

He stared into his Scotch, swirling the liquid around. 'I worked on building sites to help fund my university studies.'

He'd once thought it'd be kind of cool to renovate some old, run-down house and make it his home. But he hadn't bought that kind of house. Instead he'd bought an apartment in mint condition. He shoved the thought away. He didn't have time to play around with hammers, saws and power tools.

He crashed back to find Eve staring at him. He wasn't sure what she'd seen in his face, but he thrust out his jaw, rebelling against the sense of vulnerability that threatened to swamp him. 'I didn't know you had a grandmother who used to take you to the beach in summer.'

'I guess we didn't really know each other very well at all, did we?' she shot back.

Her mouth had never been particularly wide, and her lips weren't particularly full and generous. She didn't have a perfectly formed Cupid's bow. But he'd once told her that her mouth was the prettiest thing he'd ever seen. He still thought so. And, as he stared at it now, an ache stretched through him. She was wrong. They'd known each other in all the ways that had counted. But he didn't say that out loud. He had a feeling it would hurt her. And he had no intention of doing or saying anything that would cause her pain.

'So...' She straightened and sipped more Scotch, moderating her tone. 'What did you learn from your foray into local affairs?'

He eased back. She wasn't quizzing him for the fun of it, or to mock him. She was starting to believe he was serious in his intentions, and he wasn't screwing this up. 'Ron and his wife have two kids and one car, which is Ron's dual cab utility.'

'Yep.'

'If the primary school closes, the kids will have to catch a school bus into Byron Bay.'

'Thousands of kids catch school buses every day.'

'But if one of the kids gets sick, or has an accident at school, Ron is going to have to down tools to go and collect them.'

'Or his wife will have to take his work vehicle for the hour-long round trip. Or she finds someone in Mirror Glass Bay who can drive her there, or from whom she can borrow a car.'

'You think that's reasonable?' he demanded.

'Or they buy a second car.'

'They want neither the expense nor the environmental impact of a second car. At the moment she can race down the end of the road and walk her kid home.'

Eve didn't say a word.

'One of the other guys and his wife have his father living with them. Her parents live in Mirror Glass Bay too. The two of them are constantly juggling their timetables around taking them to an endless round of doctor appointments. But if the local clinic was to close they'd have to add an hour to their schedules to take them into Byron Bay for their appointments instead.' He shook his head. It'd make things that much more difficult for them. And those two men weren't the exception.

'They also mentioned that there's not much for local teenagers to do—there aren't many casual or part-time jobs for high-school-age kids, and even fewer full-time jobs for those who've finished school. Most are leaving town when they finish school and aren't coming back. And those who do stay are developing drug and alcohol issues.'

She nodded and he bit back a sigh. He'd hoped the men had been exaggerating but evidently they hadn't been. 'All of them were concerned about what the future held for their children.'

'Mirror Glass Bay is in danger of spiralling into obscurity and losing its amenities, and the whole town is desperate to stop it. If the primary school and clinic close, despite making it harder for those who live here it'll also discourage young families from settling here. That in turn will have a knock-on effect. Tradesmen like Ron will need to go further and further afield for work. It means businesses like mine will hire fewer and fewer people in the off season. It might only be viable to keep the bar and restaurant open in the summer.'

He glanced around. If the Mirror Glass Bay community lost this... He stiffened. 'All of those things combined would make the town too hard for people to live in. In some cases, people would have to sell up and move elsewhere.'

'Exactly.'

'And yet this place is their home.' He'd never really had a place like that. 'They love it.' *She* loved it.

'Which makes it all the more difficult to bear.'

He recalled her tone when she'd described the motel earlier. 'It's home,' she'd said. Would she have to leave if that downward spiral she'd described continued?

His hands clenched and unclenched. He'd bet she'd valiantly struggle on until her grandmother passed—and by then The Beachside would be worth next to nothing. She'd have lost her grandmother and her business. Resolution solidified in his gut. He wasn't letting that happen.

'We'll find a way to stop the decline. We'll find a way to reinvigorate your town, Eve, I promise.'

'Which brings me to the reason I asked you to join me for a drink.'

She had a plan?

He leaned towards her, all ears. 'Yes?'

'I believe I owe you an apology.'

CHAPTER FOUR

EVE COULD SCARCELY believe she'd said the words, could scarcely believe she meant them.

His brow furrowed. 'I find that highly unlikely.'

Yeah, she did too. She forced herself to look him full in the face, because she refused to be a coward about this. 'I didn't think you meant what you said.'

'That I'd help fix my mistake?'

She nodded. She'd be in danger of falling for the warmth in those clear brown eyes if she didn't know better.

But she did know better.

She pulled herself back into line. 'But it wasn't your mistake, was it? You had no control over that environmental protection order. You could've told me about it this morning and moved on... like Greamsman did.'

His head rocked back. 'You think I'm like Greamsman?'

That bugged him?

'I'm not talking on a personal level. I've no

idea if Greamsman is a barrel of laughs in his personal life or a sourpuss—whether he's faithful to his wife or if he yells at his kids. I don't even know if he is married and has kids. But in terms of what you do in your work lives you're two peas in a pod. It's the bottom line that matters, it's making money that matters.'

She had no idea why her words should make him pale. In the world he came from, it wasn't just a truth but a compliment.

'I mean, you're both very good at it,' she offered belatedly, realising she'd left that key point out, but she'd have thought it was self-evident.

He didn't say anything so she soldiered on.

'But you've made an exception here...because of me.'

He sipped his Scotch but maintained eye contact with her the entire time.

'Because you feel bad about what happened four years ago.'

'You think I shouldn't feel bad?'

He should be burning in hell for what he'd done, but she didn't say that out loud. Mirror Glass Bay needed this man. And she needed Mirror Glass Bay. If he hadn't stepped in when he had, this town would be back to square one... without resources.

Instead they now had the renowned Damon Macy on their side. *That* was the pertinent fact and the one she needed to focus on.

Four years ago, Damon had taken his two million dollars and in a bold move had invested it in a little-known start-up that had taken the world by storm. He'd sold that stock for ten times the price he'd paid for it. His two million had become a cool twenty million, allowing him to strike out on his own and form Macy Holdings. *That* was the kind of business brain Mirror Glass Bay now had access to.

It meant maybe—just maybe—they could salvage something from this mess. She wasn't asking for miracles. She just wanted to stop her town from sliding into an irrevocable decline.

'Every day for the last four years I've regretted what I did to you, Eve.'

She eased back and did what she could to stop her eyebrows from shooting up towards her hairline. 'What? You'd change what you did—undo it?'

He hesitated, and she counted three beats of her pulse before he nodded. 'Yes.'

She believed he felt bad for what he'd done. But she didn't believe he'd undo the past. She didn't believe he was sorry, regardless of what he told himself.

But, when a girl got down to brass tacks, what did it matter? She rested her elbows on the table. 'I'm going to tell you something shocking.'

His lips twisted. 'That you'd rather see Mirror Glass Bay slide into the sea than ever accept my help or have anything to do with me again, right?'

'Wow. *No!*' *What on earth...?* 'You want me to ask Cassidy to bring the whole bottle over—' she gestured to his glass '—so you can carry on sliding into some black hole of misery?'

He straightened. 'That wasn't what you were going to say?'

Nope. No siree. 'Let's be clear. I have every intention of taking advantage of your sense of guilt. I'm going to pressure you every way I know how to help my town. I've no intention of letting hurt pride, indignation or moral outrage stand in the way of what you can do here to help.'

She was pleased to see some of the darkness recede from his eyes.

No, not pleased. She rolled her shoulders. Relieved. That was all. She wasn't getting dragged back into this man's orbit—not on a personal level, where she would start to care if he was happy or not. *That* was none of her business. And she wanted to keep it that way.'

'So the shocking thing you wanted to tell me…?'

She set her shoulders. They'd deal with this and then move on. 'You did me a favour, Damon—four years ago. I'm happier now with this life—' she gestured around the restaurant and her motel '—than I'd have ever been as a high flyer in the corporate world. I love Mirror Glass Bay more than I ever loved Sydney. So you need to think again if you imagine I've spent the last four years believing my life is over, that I lost the Holy Grail and that I've settled for some lesser, second-best life. That's simply not true.'

Not that she ever expected him to understand that or appreciate the life she had now.

One long finger circled the rim of his Scotch glass. There was something magnetic, almost hypnotic, about it, reminding her of the way those fingers—and hands—had made her body come alive. Making love with him had been a transformative experience for her. And one that had never been repeated.

For him their love-making had just been a means to an end. And that still hurt four years later. But that wasn't what they were talking about. And she couldn't let her mind go there.

'You're saying I did you a favour?'

He didn't believe her. She could see it in his eyes. 'I'm saying you taught me a hard lesson.' She'd realised that she was nowhere near ruthless enough to survive in the world of finance. More to the point, she hadn't been the slightest bit interested in training herself to become that ruthless. 'The things I learnt from that lesson, the changes I decided to make to my life, have greatly increased my happiness.'

He leaned towards her. 'You're saying we're square?'

Nope, not at all. 'You did a reprehensible thing, and in doing it you deliberately broke my heart. Where do you draw the moral line on that? It's not a course of action I could condone then, and it's not one I could condone now. I'm glad you feel bad about it because it means, somewhere inside, you still have a conscience and a heart.'

Her words made him pale, but she refused to feel bad about that. 'In doing what you did, though, it forced me to look at my own choices. I realised that being some prominent and sought-after financial adviser—a high flyer with the world at my feet—wasn't what I wanted.'

He frowned and opened his mouth to speak, but she cut him off. 'I haven't regretted that decision for a single moment. *That's* what I want you to realise. *That's* what I want you to understand. So, whatever else you feel guilty about, whatever else you're beating yourself up for, you can strike that off your list.'

He stared at her from beneath hooded eyes. 'You really mean that?'

He didn't understand, but he believed her, and that was enough. He opened his mouth and again she cut him off. 'I don't want to talk about the past any more, Damon. I don't want or need to revisit it.' She didn't want to hear about how bad he felt about it. It wasn't her job to make him feel better. 'I only want to focus on the here and now and the problem at hand—how to stop Mirror Glass Bay from figuratively sliding into the sea.'

He dragged a hand down his face. 'Right.'

'Deal?' she persisted. She wanted him clear on that fact. No more discussion about their past.

Eventually he nodded. 'Do you want to shake on it?'

No. And yes. She hadn't touched him yet and she had to know. She held out her hand and he enclosed it briefly in his. The touch was short, perfunctory.

But, damn it all to hell!

She reclaimed her hand—unhurried, careful not to betray herself. She'd always had a good poker face, but she had to draw on all her vast reserves to keep it in place now. She wrapped her hand around her glass, praying it would help to cool the rush of heat that had sparked through her veins at his touch. So…that same old pull still existed, then.

Brilliant. Just brilliant.

She tossed her head. Well, fine. She simply needed to make sure they didn't touch again. *Ever.* End of story. His touch had always tempted her to wildness, had broken down her everyday guard. She couldn't let that happen if she was to survive working with him now.

She glanced at him, recognised the tightening of his jaw and her pulse went erratic. He felt it too, then—that old pull—and that didn't help. Neither one of them wanted this thing between them.

She pulled in a shaky breath. They were adults. They could ignore it.

And as an adult she could still apologise— which was what she'd been trying to do before this trip down memory lane had hijacked them. She refused to focus on the fact that he still hadn't apologised for what he'd done four years ago, even though he'd said he felt bad about it. Not once had he ever said, *I'm really sorry for what I did to you, Eve.*

Well—she squared her shoulders—she could do better than that. 'I'm sorry I didn't believe you when you said you wanted to help. It's clear that you're sincere.'

He waved her apology away. 'If you'd been forewarned that I was getting involved… And if I hadn't stumbled in, in all my glorious arrogance, thinking I had all the answers… But I did, and you rightly called me on it. I don't blame you for your scepticism, Eve. But…'

The expression in his eyes stopped her heart. 'But?'

'But you're prepared to work with me now?'

'To save Mirror Glass Bay? You bet.'

'Then I suppose the first thing we need to do is find out what kind of environmental evaluation is being done on the site, and for how long it's likely to halt work. And then discover what kind of development is more likely to be looked upon with a favourable eye. Ron and his team were telling me about some "mad hippies"— their term—who've been causing trouble, planting fake evidence and the like. If that's what has happened here, then it'll delay the development but it won't railroad it.'

True, but…

'Beck looked worried, which makes me think there's more to this.' The older woman wanted to reinvigorate the town as much as Eve did. But she wouldn't do it at the expense of the local habitat. 'But even if it is true, and that's a storm petrel breeding ground out there, it's possible that the protection order could be downgraded to a conservation order instead.'

Which would allow development at a prescribed distance from the breeding ground.

'In which case we could build…'

'A conference centre?' she suggested.

He pursed his lips and nodded. 'Weddings are a big business in Byron.'

She glanced up, surprised. He'd familiarised himself with the views of individual locals in an attempt to understand their needs and concerns. He'd attended a town meeting and, it must be said, had come up with an excellent fundraising idea; and he'd also found the time to do some research. She'd forgotten his energy. Not his drive and ambition—she remembered those vividly—but she'd forgotten exactly how much he could cram into an eight-or ten-hour day.

He tapped his fingers against his glass. 'A convention centre has definite potential. I'm looking for a place to run staff retreats. Mirror Glass Bay would be perfect.'

'Really?'

'Yep.'

Once word got out, especially given his connections, then a convention centre's success would be assured. She sucked in a breath. A convention centre would be...*perfect*.

'It won't bring in as much money or as much work as a fancy resort.'

'But it'll help. Like I said, we don't need anything crazy or over the top. We just need... *something*.' She gestured to his now empty glass. 'Would you like another?' When he shook his head, she tried to force her heart from beating so hard. 'What do you have planned for the morning?'

'Nothing yet.'

'Then I propose we go and take a good look at that parcel of land you just bought.' She forced the suggestion out before she could change her mind.

'Excellent plan.'

She gathered up the glasses and stood. 'It's time for me to grab some shut-eye. I'll see you tomorrow...around nine?'

He rose and pointed. 'Here?'

'Or Reception.'

He bade her goodnight and she took their glasses to the bar and waved goodnight to Cassidy, before letting herself out of the same doors as Damon had. They led out into the internal quadrangle with its gardens and she ambled for several yards, relishing the stillness of a quiet night.

'Dolores?' she called out softly. 'Come on, Dolly, where are you?'

'Who's Dolores?'

She whipped round to find Damon sitting at one of the picnic tables.

'Sorry, I didn't mean to startle you. I stopped to admire the sky.'

She glanced upward automatically. The night sky was amazing here. It had mesmerised her when she'd first arrived too.

A loud meow carried on the still night air. Eve lifted a finger. 'That's Dolores—my cat.' She peered into the darkness, which admittedly wasn't all that dark, given the safety lights in the garden and the light from the moon and the stars. 'Where are you, Dolly?'

Another two meows and she finally located her. She was on the balcony of Damon's room. Eve planted her hands on her hips. 'What are you doing up there, miss?' Had she snuck into Damon's room and inadvertently been locked in? She'd be starving!

'I…uh…'

Damon came to stand beside her. The smell of the boardroom had started to dissolve, replaced instead with the scent of cotton and soap, the leather of his steel-capped work boots and salt-scented breezes. A definite improvement.

He gestured to his balcony. 'That's my fault. She came to visit earlier and curled up on my bed for a nap. I didn't have the heart to wake her. I left a dish of water for her. When I got home again in the afternoon she didn't seem inclined to leave. I left all the doors open, but…'

'You didn't think to pick her up and put her out?'

One shoulder lifted. 'It seemed a bit mean.'

She blinked.

'I went to that little supermarket and bought her a tin of tuna.'

He'd fed her cat? This man, who was considered a corporate shark in boardroom negotiations, hadn't had the heart to put her cat outside? And had then gone out of his way to buy a can of tuna to feed said cat?

'The company's been nice,' he muttered.

She tried to hold back a smile. 'Well, I'm afraid whether you enjoy her company or not you're now stuck with her for the duration of your stay.

She will refuse to budge—especially if you keep feeding her tuna.'

'You won't mind?'

'Absolutely not.' She turned to face him fully. 'But we have one golden rule where Dolores is concerned. She's fifteen, which is old in cat years. She spends most of her time sleeping in the sun. But she's still a cat with a cat's instincts. We keep her indoors at night—there's too much nocturnal wildlife she can hunt and harm.'

'Okay.'

'She'll test your limits—meow and make a fuss.'

'I promise to keep her in. I won't let her out till the morning.'

'And if she isn't in your room one night you need to let someone know—me or Cassidy—so we can hunt for her. We inherited Dolores with the motel and she divides her time between my grandmother's unit, Cassidy's place and my place.' She pointed to her unit above Reception.

Just for a moment, their gazes caught and clung. His gaze lowered to her lips and a low thrum started up inside her. Temptation swelled. It'd be so easy...

No!

She reefed her gaze away but forced her legs to hold firm. With a deep breath she met his gaze again—forced her eyes to narrow and pulled her lips into unsmiling lines.

'I want to make this clear, Damon. We're not revisiting the past in any way, shape or form. It's probably not something that needs stating—' like hell it wasn't '—but I want us crystal-clear on that point.'

He took a step back. 'Absolutely! I would never…'

He shook his head, his nostrils flaring, and then he smiled, but she sensed the effort it cost him.

'Eve, I appreciate your frankness. It's always wise for a woman to set boundaries she's comfortable with. I promise not to overstep them.'

Good, she told herself. That was…*good*.

She edged away from him, feeling the magnetic pull of the man but determined to ignore it—determined he shouldn't become aware of her weakness. She had no idea if he'd exploit it, and she had no intention of finding out. But as she walked away she found a smile touching her lips.

Hot damn!

The man had fed the cat. He evidently had a weakness or two of his own.

Damon was ready and waiting on the dot of nine outside Reception the next morning.

Inside Eve exchanged a couple of words with her receptionist and then joined him. She wore jeans, hiking boots and a long-sleeved shirt. Everything was covered, as if she were trying to hide her body from view. His gut clenched. She'd made it clear last night that she wasn't interested in him. Was she worried he wouldn't keep his word?

With one comprehensive sweep of her eyes, she raked him up and down, and his gut clenched in an entirely different way. 'Are you wearing sunscreen?' she demanded without preamble.

It took a moment for her words to penetrate the fog surrounding his brain, but when they did he wanted to laugh. Not a mirthful belly laugh, but a scornful laugh, directed solely at his own over-inflated sense of self. Her covering up had nothing to do with him. If yesterday hadn't proved beyond all doubt that she'd moved on from the events of four years ago, then this moment now hammered another nail in the coffin of his vanity.

'Slathered in the stuff,' he assured her. He'd spent the last four years in a hell of his own making, while she...

She'd chalked it up to experience and moved on.

'Bug spray?' she asked.

He shook his head. Insect repellent hadn't oc-curred to him. In Sydney the mosquitoes and flies were only a problem in summer.

She disappeared back into Reception, emerg-ing a moment later to toss him a small tube of cream. 'We have wetland areas around here, and when you combine that with the warm autumn weather…'

She didn't want him getting eaten alive by bugs. It was only a little thing, but he'd take whatever crumbs she offered. And, if that made him pathetic, he didn't care.

'Thanks.' He applied the stuff and then put the tube in the pocket of his cargo shorts in case they should need more later.

Surveyors had pegged out the perimeter of the site with wooden stakes and plastic tape, while an access road ran through the middle of the four-teen-hectare site. The southern boundary shared a border with residential homes. To the west and north it bordered National Park, and to the east it had direct access to the beach.

Eve planted her hands on her hips and turned a slow circle. 'This is such a great location.'

Her jeans fitted her like a glove and it made this mouth go dry. He forced his gaze away, chiding himself for noticing. 'It's a *pretty* location,' he corrected. 'It's only going to be great if we can develop it.' He kept his gaze trained on the land. 'If you were a white-bellied storm petrel, where would you make a nest?'

'They're seabirds so…near the water, but protected from the strong winds we can get here, I guess. What do you think?'

He nodded. It sounded like she'd read the same research articles he had.

They started in the north-eastern corner and worked their way westwards. Nothing. They swept back again. They kept that up for an hour. Eventually he pulled to a halt. 'Look, Greamsman was about to start clearing the lot, right? That means he'd have already been granted DA approval, which means someone from the local council had to have come out here to assess the site.'

'Unless he bent the rules…paid someone off.'

It happened, but it was risky. Greamsman had a ruthless streak a mile wide, but he wasn't an idiot. 'Let's say it was assessed and that nothing was found. If the nesting ground is just outside my boundaries, that would still impact on what I can do with the site, right? I could still be slapped with a stop-work notice while further investigations were carried out.'

They started scouting through the National Park to the north. And found Beck. 'I had a feeling I might see you two out here today,' she said by way of greeting.

'Have you found anything?' Eve asked. She wore a cap that shaded her face, but he saw the way her gaze sharpened beneath its brim.

'Come with me.'

He fell into step behind both women when Beck gestured for them to follow her.

'Here,' she said, gesturing around. 'I've found a dozen nests in total so far, but I think there'll be more. From what I can tell, though, these are the ones closest to your boundary.'

He glanced back the way they'd come. 'So...in all likelihood this'll mean a conservation order rather than a protection order.' That would mean, within certain parameters, he could still develop the site.

'As long as you can guarantee a generous green corridor on your northern boundary.'

He pulled the site plans from his pocket. He and Eve consulted them, pointing out likely new perimeters for any building work.

'That's not all I found.' Beck heaved out a sigh. 'There's also evidence of a small squirrel-glider colony here.' She pointed to a spot on his western boundary.

'Which is great news for the squirrel glider,' Eve said glumly.

'Because we love our native fauna and want to protect it where we can,' Beck said just as glumly.

'But our convention centre is becoming smaller and smaller,' he finished for them.

'But not impossible, right?'

Eve bit her lip, worry darkening her eyes. In that moment Damon swore again to make this right somehow. He injected confidence into his voice. 'Not impossible at all.'

The thing was, if he really wanted to shore up this town's viability he was going to need more than a single-pronged approach.

'What? You're looking worried. What's wrong?'

Eve's questions hurtled him back with a thump. He shook his head. 'Nothing. Just thinking.' He turned to Beck. 'You'll get your report in ASAP?'

She nodded.

'In the meantime, I'm going to contact an architect I know. He's making a name for himself with his environmentally sympathetic designs. By the time he gets back to me with some ideas, the relevant authorities should have rubber-stamped the necessary covenants and lifted the temporary embargo.' Especially if he lit a fire under the necessary authorities. 'Once that happens, building can start.'

'My vote is still for the research centre,' Beck grumbled.

Eve patted her on the shoulder. 'Keep trying, Beck. Keep lobbying for all the government grants you can, and petitioning universities. You'll get your research centre one day.'

They left Beck to her inspection and started back towards the motel. 'What did you mean by that?'

She pulled her cap off and ran a hand through her hair, the blonde highlights glinting in the autumn sunshine. Everything about her breathed warmth and vigour. Just walking beside her made him feel happier, more content, more relaxed than he'd felt in…

Not just four years but *forever*.

'Beck has been petitioning Parks and Wildlife, local council and state government for years to set up a research centre here, and it sounds as if her case is starting to grow. Not only do we have an isolated koala population, but now a squirrel-glider colony and a white-bellied storm petrel breeding ground.'

A research centre made sense.

He glanced at his watch. 'Are you busy for the next hour or so? I have a guy coming from Byron Bay to show me around some of the warehouses in the industrial estate.'

She glanced up so quickly, her gaze so intent, he nearly stumbled. 'Why?'

They halted beside his car and he widened his stance, trying to regain his balance, forcing himself to focus on what mattered to her—and that *wasn't* his physical reaction.

'Okay, full disclosure here.' He pulled in a breath. 'I think it's wise to have a back-up plan. Mirror Glass Bay should *not* be relying on your motel and my hypothetical conference centre for its continuing financial viability.'

He punctuated each point with a stabbing finger, then realised he might be coming across as too intense and pulled his hand back to his side. 'What if your motel burns down? What if an even better conference centre gets built nearby, or people decide beach weddings are passé, or—'

'Or there's another down-turn in the market.' She sighed.

'I have no idea what potential these warehouses hold, but I figure it can't hurt to look. And two heads are better than one.'

'Especially when they're our heads.' Her lips twisted, almost in self-mockery. 'You have an inside track into the corporate world while I've got the skinny on the local community.'

Her eyes suddenly gleamed and he sensed her mind racing the way it used to in the old days, whenever she'd discovered an exciting new investment opportunity. Was she really no longer interested in the financial markets or following stock and futures prices? She'd said that she was happy with her life now and he had no reason to disbelieve her. But it didn't stop him from wondering.

The tour of the five empty premises that were located between the small work-gear clothing factory, with its tiny outlet, a panel beaters and the rural fire brigade quarters ranged in size from a huge site, that could be turned to any number of uses, to a small office block and everything in between. After their inspection, he and Eve hunkered down at a picnic table in the gardens of The Beachside with their laptops, the local newspapers and some sandwiches. Best office ever.

'Right,' he said after forty solid minutes of research. 'I'm dreaming big. I want this guy to build his boats here.'

He swung his laptop round, and her mouth fell open, not in surprise but in chagrin. 'Hot damn. Really? It'd be a hell of a coup.'

She then turned her laptop towards him. 'This is what I was thinking. Craft beer is huge at the moment—and cider.'

She had a list of equipment needed and the specifications required for such an operation, as well as the names of all the local brewers.

He tapped a finger against the table top. 'How are we going to do this?' They could cold call these guys or…

'Your ship-building guy is having a huge party at his house in Byron Bay a week Saturday.' She flipped over the pages of the local paper and pointed to an article in the social pages.

Perfect.

'I'll find a way to get us in.'

CHAPTER FIVE

EVE FASTENED THE leg rope of her board around her ankle and headed straight into the surf. At 7:00 a.m., the beach was utter perfection. The sun had slipped above the horizon, painting the sea gold and orange, and, untouched by even a breath of breeze, the water looked like satin. Out the back a perfect swell built to curling sets of breakers that would allow her to practise her rail-to-rail surfing and bottom turns to her heart's content.

She waved to another couple of riders—evenly spaced and too far away to drop in on each other. They waved back, no one shouting out a greeting, no one wanting to break the spell of the morning quiet.

It was nearly June—nearly winter in the southern hemisphere—but the water temperature was twenty-four degrees Celsius. Some mornings she wanted to weep with gratitude and happiness.

She caught waves and tried to lose herself to the magical sensation of being buoyed by a force so much greater than herself, one that could never wholly be predicted.

But the same concerns, and the same face, that had kept her tossing and turning for the last three nights kept intruding into her thoughts. She'd manage to push those thoughts from her mind and catch a wave, only to have them reappear a moment later when paddling back out to catch the next wave.

Exhausting.

She was tempted to head back in, but sheer bloody-mindedness had her determined to stay at her usual morning post for her traditional forty minutes.

She sat on her board and glanced around, and something inside her settled. *This* was the life she loved. She didn't want to be anywhere else. She loved Mirror Glass Bay. She loved her motel. She loved her community.

And yet none of that changed the fact that when she'd been scouring the paper and Internet for local investment opportunities two days ago something had come alive inside her. She'd loved rising to that challenge. She scrubbed both hands back over her hair. It didn't mean she wanted to return to the corporate world, though. She couldn't think of anything worse. And that was the truth.

She caught a wave to shore and, with her board tucked under her arm, walked up the beach to where she'd left her towel. Young Pru—a local youngster Eve had befriended and taken under her wing...or had *tried* to take under her wing—was sitting on it, but she leapt up to hand it over as Eve approached.

Eve's heart started to pound when she saw who sat beside Pru.

Damon.

He stared at her and his jaw dropped. 'That was *you* out there?'

Pru grinned, taking a seat on the sand. 'I knew he thought you were a guy, so I just let him keep thinking it.'

She forced herself to laugh. Damon had been watching her surf? She was glad she hadn't known that when she'd been out there.

'You...you rat!' Damon feigned outrage. But then he grinned and shook his head, glancing back at Eve. 'You're really good.'

A man's praise shouldn't warm her. It shouldn't matter.

It *didn't* matter.

'I didn't know you surfed.'

'Eve learned when she was a kid—my age—but she was pretty crap when she first came here.'

That made her laugh for real. 'Thank you, Pru.'

'Yeah, but you know you're really, *really* good now.'

The wistfulness that crossed the young girl's

face made Eve's heart burn. So much about Pru made her heart burn. 'Hot chocs up at The Beachside?'

Damon blinked but followed them into the café section of the motel. A waitress came bustling up with three steaming mugs of hot chocolate. Eve watched Damon wrestle with his curiosity—he wanted to ask questions, lots of questions—and she was almost proud of him when he bit them back and just watched, submitting to taking events as they came. It'd be an alien concept for him.

'You should auction surfing lessons at the fundraiser,' Pru said. 'I'd bid on them. I have thirty-eight dollars and fifty cents. Do you think that'd be enough?'

'As I expect you'd be the only bidder, it should be more than enough.'

The smile dropped from Pru's face. 'Except I don't have a board, so it wouldn't matter even if I was the highest bidder.'

'We'd find a way around that—we could borrow one.' Pru's face lit up again. Eve nearly offered to give her lessons for free but managed to stop herself at the last minute. 'You really think I should auction off lessons?'

Pru nodded vehemently. Damon watched them both with a still intensity she found impossible to ignore and that sent her pulse fluttering in the strangest way.

'All right, then. I'll do it.'

Pru gave a cheer.

'You know,' Damon said, 'it occurs to me that we should run a raffle in conjunction with the auction. And Pru has hit on the perfect prize—a surfboard. What do you think?'

Pru's eyes went wide. 'I'd buy a ticket. And Mum would too.'

He grimaced. 'I'd need some help choosing the right surfboard, though. I know nothing about surfing. While you...' he addressed Pru '...know everything.'

'You want *me* to help you choose the surfboard?'

'You and Eve.'

'We'd be delighted to, wouldn't we, Pru?' Eve said promptly, even though not twenty minutes ago she'd been reminding herself to spend less time with Damon, not more.

Pru nodded, her eyes shining as she finished her hot chocolate. She glanced at the clock on the wall and wrinkled her nose. 'I've gotta go to school now. Bye.'

They waved the young girl off.

'What's the deal with her?' Damon asked once she was out of earshot. 'She seems lonely. Reminded me of myself as a kid.'

Had Damon had a lonely childhood? He hadn't talked much about it four years ago—had always deflected her questions. She'd always thought he'd tell her more once they'd been together a bit longer—that she'd earn his trust. She'd been prepared to wait. But things hadn't turned out the way she'd thought they would.

She pushed the thought away.

'Pru is what my gran's generation called a latchkey kid. Her mum is a single mother and is working three part-time jobs just to make ends meet. She's a nice woman but she's doing it tough. She doesn't spend anywhere near enough time with her daughter as either one of them would like.'

'And she can't afford to buy her daughter a surfboard.'

'Nope.' She glanced at him and then swiped her finger through what remained of her hot-chocolate foam and stuck it in her mouth. 'You know you can't rig that raffle, Damon. You can't make sure that she wins the surfboard.'

'But if she buys a ticket she's in with a chance, right?'

A slim one. She was swiping her finger through more foam when he suddenly leaned across the table, pinning her with merciless eyes.

'Why didn't you offer to give her surf lessons for free? That seems like the kind of thing that should happen in a place like this.'

Was he disappointed in her? The thought bemused her.

'It took me weeks to talk her into having a

hot chocolate with me, and she only does it be-cause I told her there's no one else to talk to about surfing—or that everyone here is too busy to have a drink with me in the mornings. I once asked her if she'd like to have some breakfast. I didn't see her for a week after that.'

He sat back and she popped her finger in her mouth. His gaze immediately darted away and her stomach started to churn. She pushed her mug aside.

'Pru is insanely sensitive when it comes to anything she thinks might be charity. Which is why you can't buy her a surfboard.'

His lips thinned into a grim line and he gave a hard nod. 'It's not uncommon among poor kids. They don't have anything except their pride.'

'Were you and your family poor when you were growing up?' She couldn't believe the ques-tion had slipped out, but there was something in his face. And it might help to explain why he'd sold her down the river. It might explain why success was so important to him.

Her spine suddenly stiffened. What was she doing? His answer didn't matter. It changed noth-ing.

'Sorry, don't answer that. It's none of my busi-ness.'

'We were dirt poor,' he said. 'My mum was a single mother too until she married my stepfather when I was fourteen. Things got easier after that.'

She stared at him. It was more than he'd ever told her in those few months when they'd been seeing each other. She wanted to get up and walk away—she didn't want to hear his story—but she didn't have it in her to be that rude, that heartless. And it would be heartless. He had shadows in his eyes—she had no intention of asking about them, but she couldn't leave him alone with them.

'Considering your humble beginnings, you certainly reached exalted heights. You must be pleased with all you've achieved.'

She didn't ask him if his parents were proud of him because she knew how complicated family could be. She didn't ask him if he was proud of himself because he'd stomped on her on his way up that ladder of success—and she didn't want to hear him admit that he thought it had been a worthwhile thing to do.

'My success makes me feel safe in a way I never felt as a kid.'

Her chest burned. Her temples started to throb.

'Your family were very different.'

She nodded. 'I was lucky. My parents were both professionals—very successful. I'm not talking Vaucluse area of Sydney kind of money, here, but I grew up in a beachside suburb in Sydney. I could walk to the beach.'

'"Successful"?' His lips twisted. 'Isn't that code for never being at home because they were always at work?'

The latent sympathy beneath his words had her gripping her empty mug too tight. She loosened her grasp and eased back in her chair. 'Don't go putting me in the same category as you and Pru. My parents might not have spent much time with me.' It was hard to understand why they'd ever had a child. 'But there was plenty of money for surf lessons, surfboards, dance classes and the best university money could buy. Money does make a difference—a big difference. I entered the workforce debt free and with all of my ideals intact.' Back then she been completely unaware of her own privilege.

'With the weight of your parents' expectations on your shoulders, no doubt. It was why you were so determined to prove yourself at Spellman and Spelman wasn't it?'

'What does any of that matter now?'

He searched her face. She concentrated on keeping her expression smooth and unruffled. 'It doesn't,' he finally said.

'Whichever way you look at it, my route to Spellman and Spelman was easier than yours. And my childhood was easier than Pru's as well. I had my grandma and my school friends. I wasn't lonely as a kid.'

He leaned forward, intense again. 'Pru doesn't have school friends?'

Her heart chugged, burned and did things she had a feeling it'd be better to not understand.

'It's a small school. The kids are generally pretty good to each other. But Pru's two best friends left last year—their parents had to move for work.'

His fingers drummed against the table. 'It all comes back to revitalising the town.' His gaze sharpened. 'These are reasons it matters so much to you.'

She fought the automatic roll of her eyes and a sarcastic, *Duh!* 'Yes.'

His lips twitched, as if he'd read that struggle. 'Then you'll be pleased to know that I've managed to get us on the guest list to the Sorensen party.'

She straightened. Simon Sorensen was a yacht-building tycoon. 'How did you manage that?'

'Saturday, seven p.m., black tie. You in?'

'Yes!' She wouldn't get such access to so many local business people and wheeler-dealers again. She didn't know how Damon had managed it, what strings he'd pulled, but she'd be an idiot to knock back an opportunity like this. 'I better dust off one of my old frocks.' She stretched her neck first one way and then the other. 'You wouldn't happen to know who else is on the guest list?'

'Of course I do. I'll email the list to you.' He stood. 'I'll talk to you later, Eve.'

Cassidy came up the moment he left and took his vacated seat. 'Are you really going to a party with him?'

Cassidy had been eavesdropping! Eve shook herself upright. 'Of course I am. It's too good an opportunity to miss. If I can make just a few local connections...' She rolled her eyes at Cassidy's expression. 'Cass, this isn't a date. It's business.'

'I know that's what you're telling yourself, but you need to be careful, Evie. I have a feeling that man is your kryptonite. None of us should be playing with kryptonite.'

'Kryptonite doesn't hurt mortals.'

'We're not mortals, Eve. We're superwomen.'

That made her laugh. 'Sorry, my mistake.'

Cassidy leaned forward, serious again. 'Be careful.'

She sobered too. 'I will be. I promise. I know spending time with him is dangerous. But he'll be gone again before we know it.'

Worry flooded Cassidy's eyes. 'You still find him attractive.'

'C'mon, Cass, the guy's hot. And I'm not dead.'

'Kryptonite,' her friend intoned darkly.

'But all I have to do to counter the danger is remember what he did. And any tiny hint of temptation that raises its head will be shot down in flames. Don't worry, Cass, I'm not getting involved with that man ever again. I promise.' She clasped her friend's hand briefly. 'Now, I better go have a shower and get down here to help with the morning rush.'

* * *

That Saturday night, Damon could barely breathe when Eve removed her wrap to reveal the stunning dress she wore. Not that he noticed the dress so much as *her*.

Colour mounted high on her cheekbones when she glanced at him. He kicked himself mentally and smoothed out his face, hoping like hell it hid the heat in his eyes. She'd made it clear that she wasn't interested in pursuing any kind of physical thing with him.

He respected that, and only a jerk would mount any kind of protest and make her feel uncomfortable.

And he wasn't a masochist. He wanted her—everything inside him clamoured to be near her. But he wanted all of her, not just a scrap or crumb. And he would never have all of her—she'd never allow it. She'd never trust him with her heart again. And he didn't blame her.

So he smoothed out his frown and forced a smile. 'You look stunning.'

Did he imagine the relief in her eyes? 'You already said that, Damon.'

He tucked her hand into the crook of his elbow. 'That was merely customary politeness, what a man is supposed to say when he arrives to collect a woman—any woman,' he hastened to add. 'This is proper appreciation.' She wore a calf-length dress of extraordinarily fine silk in a warm buttery yellow that clung to her every curve. It's low cowl neck made his mouth water.

'This was the last dress I bought when I was still living in Sydney.' She named a well-known Australian designer. 'Terribly extravagant, but I couldn't resist. It's the first time I've worn it.'

'Whatever you paid, it was worth it.'

She laughed and some of the tension drained out of him. His earlier ogling hadn't left her feeling indelibly uncomfortable. He'd make sure to stay on his guard against such slips for the rest of the evening.

She glanced at him. 'You're not looking too bad yourself. You always did a tux proud.'

Her words made his heart hammer, ache and burn all at the same time. 'I'd want to do this one proud.' He made his voice wry and self-deprecating. 'It's tailor made.' He'd had it couriered up from Sydney. 'Whatever your dress cost, I bet this cost twice as much.'

She laughed again and this time he found he could manage a grin. 'Ready to work the room?'

'Absolutely.'

The Sorensen mansion—probably more of a complex—was strategically perched on the Byron Bay headland. Below were spectacular ocean views that were incredible at night and would therefore be ten times more impressive during the day.

The open-plan living area was filled with people. French doors opened out to a terrace and the most spectacular pool and gardens. He let out a breath. The Sorensens' neighbours were movie stars and celebrities, and more than a few of them had chosen to grace the party with their presence.

'Nice,' Eve murmured at his elbow, though he noted she was staring at the pool rather than the apparently swoon-worthy film star who'd just strode across their line of vision.

He took two glasses of champagne from a proffered tray and handed her one. She touched her glass to his and just for a moment their gazes clung.

She blinked and broke the moment. 'See the man over there?' He glanced to where she indicated. 'That's Mr Dalton...a local brewer.' Damon filed the information away.

'And that man over there is our host.' He nodded in the direction of the luxury-yacht builder.

She stared. 'I think you should take Dalton while I take Mr Sorensen.'

'Divide and conquer?'

'You bet.'

He feigned outrage. 'You just want the kudos of closing the bigger deal and leaving me with the small fry.'

'Mr Dalton is not small fry! He's also a fan of Australian soccer—he's thinking of buying a club in the national league. From memory, that was your thing too, right?'

He feigned further outrage. 'It's called *football*, not soccer.'

It was an old argument that had her grinning. 'Whatever. But I have a point of contact with Mr Sorensen—I once had a cruise around Sydney harbour in the *Joyful Jade*.'

He eased back in genuine admiration. 'That was his first big yacht.' That was when the Sorensen brand had become synonymous with luxury and quality.

'I know. And it's an in.'

She'd done her homework but so had he. 'You have an in with the Daltons too. His goddaughter is one of your housekeeping staff.'

It was her jaw that dropped this time.

'And he's a big reader of mystery novels—his favourite author is Agatha Christie. You once told me that you spent your summers re-reading your favourite Agatha Christie books.'

She blinked. 'You remember that?'

In the same way she'd remembered that he was a football fanatic. 'Sure I do.' He spoke the words lightly enough, but the atmosphere between them threatened to turn tense. He made himself gaze back out at the crowd.

Keep it light. Don't make her feel uncomfortable.

'While I'm considering buying a luxury yacht.'

'Ah, so you want me to take Mr Dalton while you have a shot with Mr Sorensen.'

He shook his head. 'I don't think divide and conquer is our best strategy. I'm thinking that together we make a crack team. Why halve our power and impact if we don't have to? There's time for us to chat with both the Sorensens and the Daltons.'

'A joint charm offensive?'

He grinned down at her. 'Precisely.'

She grinned back. 'Game on.'

The fire in her eyes did something to him. She couldn't hide how much she enjoyed the thrill of the chase, even if she wasn't aware of it herself.

They greeted their host and hostess first. Mr Sorensen's eyes narrowed when they rested on Damon. 'I'm intrigued to know what you're doing in town, Mr Macy. Kevin Greamsman has been saying some…interesting things about you.'

'The name's Damon. And you shouldn't believe everything you hear. Come and find me when your host duties are less urgent and you can have the story straight from the horse's mouth.'

'I'm going to do that,' the other man promised.

Damon and Eve slowly worked their way around the room until they'd reached the Daltons' circle. Introductions were made. 'I'm feeling a little envious,' Damon said to the other man, who was probably twenty years his senior. 'I hear you're thinking of buying one of the football teams.'

'Not exactly. I'm trying to get a syndicate

of businessmen together—a joint-ownership scheme. And I'm actually pushing the national soccer federation to expand the league to include a team from the Gold Coast. Things are looking promising.' He sent Damon a cheeky grin. 'I don't suppose you'd be interested in coming on board?'

A little over a week ago, he'd have said no. But that was before he'd promised to get himself a life.

'ROI is going to be…well…probably non-existent,' the older man confessed.

'But what price do you put on the enjoyment of owning a team in the national league and sitting in a corporate box to enjoy the games?'

'That's what I keep telling Barbara here. What do you think, Eve?'

She rolled her eyes at Barbara Dalton. 'It sounds like every boyhood dream come true.'

Everyone laughed. 'Keep me in the loop, Garry,' Damon told the other man.

Talk turned to recent movie releases. Garry Dalton turned to them. 'Have you seen the latest Agatha Christie adaptation?'

Eve wrinkled her nose. 'I don't know if I dare risk it. The movies are never as good as the books.'

Damon smiled as the two started discussing the ins and outs of the book and film, and he contented himself making small talk with Barbara.

Usually he found such events onerous but that wasn't the case tonight. Barbara had a passion for animal welfare and was heavily involved in the local dog shelter. 'I had a rescue dog as a kid,' he said. Which strictly speaking wasn't true. The dog had been a stray that he'd taken home with him and had somehow managed to feed. Most of the time. 'He was the best friend I ever had.' That much was true.

'Pets are great for children,' she agreed. Her eyes suddenly gleamed. 'You wouldn't be interested in owning another dog, would you, Damon?'

'Not for myself. At least, not at the moment. But…' Pru's face popped into his mind. 'I might know someone.' He grimaced. 'Dogs can be expensive, though, right? Vet bills and vaccinations.'

Her gaze sharpened. 'We're also looking for foster carers for our dogs. When someone fosters a dog, all of the dog's expenses continue to be covered by the organisation.'

Would Pru be interested in that? 'Do you have a card?'

She handed it to him. 'Ring me if you have any questions.' At the same time Garry Dalton swung back to them.

'Eve here owns the motel that our Danielle works at, Barb. And between us we've come up with a grand idea—murder mystery weekends at the motel! Isn't that the most splendid idea you've ever heard?'

The older man's enthusiasm was infectious and Damon found himself grinning. *Well played, Eve!* He had to resist the impulse to reach across and high-five her.

They discussed the idea for a while, Eve moving to the side when some of the women asked about the stunning necklet that she wore. He caught snatches of the conversation.

'Mirror Glass Bay resident…'

'Self-taught…'

'Freelance…'

'I'll send you her details…'

And then, as if the thought had only just occurred to her, she said, 'Hey, we're having a fundraising auction for koala conservation in four weeks' time. And this particular jeweller is donating a really lovely piece for the cause. You should all come. There's going to be a fabulous band—Damon is pulling some strings, but their name will make your mouths drop when we finally get to announce it. It should be a lot of fun.'

The woman was a one-man band. She was amazing. She hadn't hit up a single one of them, the cream of Byron Bay society, to donate anything. These men and women were used to petitions on their pockets and resources, but she hadn't attempted to appeal to their better natures or their consciences. Instead she'd promised them a great night out and the opportunity to score a unique piece of jewellery.

'So spill, Damon,' Simon Sorensen said, sauntering across to him. 'What are you really doing in town?' All the other men in the circle immediately honed in on the conversation. Damon didn't kid himself. How he handled the next five to ten minutes was going to be crucial to Operation Mirror Glass Bay.

'Besides catching up with old friends?' He indicated Eve, who he knew was listening but was pretending not to be. 'I'm finding Mirror Glass Bay a bit of an…under-used resource. There's potential there that I wouldn't mind harnessing. I've been after a place to run team-building retreats for a while now. Somewhere quiet and out of the way in an inspirational location.'

'Ah, the Greamsman site.'

'My site now—an ideal beach-front parcel of land surrounded on two sides by national park that can't be built on. And the price…' He shook his head. 'It's impossible to get beachside land further south at those kinds of prices. Greamsman was crazy to sell to me. The environmental embargo scared the silly goose off.'

'That's not the story he tells.'

Damon grinned. 'Of course it's not.' Sorensen wasn't a man who could be easily influenced, and Damon had no intention of lying to him. 'Greamsman only had one vision for that site. If

he'd expanded his thinking outside the square…
But he didn't.'

Sorensen still didn't look convinced, but
Damon needed to convince this man that he
would be a safe bet to work with—for Eve's sake.
'Compare Greamsman's staff retention rates to
mine. That reveals the differences in our business
cultures and approaches. Carrots work better
than sticks, gentlemen. It's the perks and conditions that Macy Holdings offers its employees
that attracts and keeps the best staff.'

'And being offered a week or two each year to
enjoy the sun and sand when you're working on
so-called team building is a nice perk.'

'And in a place like Mirror Glass Bay, where
there's no real nightlife to distract the staff,' Dalton added.

Damon didn't answer immediately, just let the
beginnings of a smile tickle the corners of his
mouth.

'Studies show that relaxation and the positive
ions from moving water are conducive to creativity and problem-solving.' He sipped his champagne, still the same glass he'd taken when he
and Eve had first walked in. 'It's been working
for me…so let's hope it works for my team.'

'Working for you?' Sorensen pressed.

'There's an old industrial area on the way
into town—a bit run-down now, with over half
the warehouses either sitting vacant or under-

utilised. There's potential there for the right investor.'

The women joined the group. They were as curious as the men—and, as several of them had business degrees and were active business partners with their spouses, he was only surprised they'd not joined the conversation sooner. He suspected the local rumour mill had been working overtime this last week.

'It has occurred to me recently that all work and no play makes for a dull life.'

Eve's eyes felt like a physical presence on his skin, but he didn't turn to meet them.

'It's why I might be persuaded to buy into your football team, Garry. Eve called it a boyhood dream come true, but I don't see that there's anything wrong with that. Owning a brewery comes under that same umbrella.'

'The market is already flooded here,' Dalton said promptly.

He laughed. 'Which is exactly what you would say to deter new competition.'

Dalton rubbed a hand across his chin. 'However, I am looking to expand my operations. I'm not looking to move my entire operations to brand-new premises, mind—it currently makes no sense to do that—but if there's something suitable on this industrial estate of yours…?'

Damon nodded slowly. 'We should talk.'

'Darling.' Valerie Sorensen slipped a hand

through her husband's arm. 'This sounds like an interesting opportunity.'

Eve turned to him. 'Valerie was just telling us that Simon is diversifying into smaller craft—jet skis and skiffs.'

'I was hoping to buy a site not too far from my shipyard, but the price isn't right yet.'

'And the owner is an odious man,' his wife said. 'Look, Damon, why don't you and Eve, and Barbara and Garry, all come to dinner on Wednesday night? We can have a good old natter about it all over steak and salad.'

They all agreed and settled on a time. Eve sent him a grin that made him feel as if he could fly.

'I can't believe how much we accomplished,' Eve said on the way home in the car later that night.

Even in the darkness he could see the way her eyes danced. Excitement shimmered off her in waves; she could barely keep still in her seat.

'You won Dalton over with your murder-mystery weekend idea.'

'It was his idea.'

'Correction—you let him think it was his idea. I was there, remember? I heard what was said.'

She waved that away. 'You won both Barbara and Valerie over with your interest in the dog shelter.'

'How'd you know about that?'

'Barbara told us about it when you were talking about team-building retreats with the men.' She turned in her seat to face him. 'Who were you thinking of getting a dog for? I can't have a dog at the motel, it'd—'

'Pru.' He told her about the foster care option and how that might suit Pru's mother's tight budget.

She nodded slowly. 'That's a really nice idea.' She sent him a sharp glance. 'You better be careful, Damon. You're in danger of losing your reputation as a shark.'

He didn't care. Not when it put such a spark in her eyes.

He drove down Beach Street towards her motel and blinked at all the lights that blazed from the restaurant and bar. 'I didn't know you had a function on tonight.'

'We don't. This is called small town nosiness. Word will have circulated about where we were headed tonight and what we were up to.'

Really? He wasn't sure what to say. His stomach started to clench. 'Well, at least it's good for business, I suppose.'

CHAPTER SIX

Eve stared at the light spilling from The Beach-side, at the smiling faces and general laughter inside, and something hitched in her chest.

These were her people.

This was her home.

What she and Damon had done tonight…

You haven't closed any deals yet.

But they *had* set wheels in motion. Not just one but several. Damon was right. They shouldn't be relying on only one or two sources of local industry to provide revenue and employment opportunities in the area. Not if they wanted to maintain and eventually enhance Mirror Glass Bay's infrastructure.

She turned back to Damon. 'Thank you for everything you're doing and have already done.' She was reaping untold rewards from the bad turn he'd done her four years ago. It'd be churlish not to acknowledge that.

And tonight she wasn't feeling churlish. Tonight, she felt euphoric. 'I want you to know I really appreciate it. The whole town appreciates it.'

He shook his head, not smiling. 'It's the least that I could do.'

'No.' She wondered how his eyes could look so vibrant in the darkness of the car. 'You're doing far more than Greamsman would've done. And you're doing far more than you ever had to. I wouldn't have blamed you for walking away.'

The light in his eyes darkened, became more subdued. 'Are you so sure about that?'

She thought about it and then grimaced. 'I'd have blamed you for getting involved. *Until* I'd found out about the stop-work notice.' But he hadn't walked away. He was doing what he promised—he was fixing things.

Neither of them made reference to the past. But the past suddenly didn't seem to matter so much. 'Come on.' She hitched her head in the direction of the bar. 'Let's go join in the fun.' She didn't want the night to end.

'You're saying the whole town knows we went to that party?'

'Looks like it.' She leaned back in her seat and folded her arms when he didn't move. He really didn't get it, did he? 'Who did you mention the party to?'

'Ron—but only in passing. I didn't make a big thing about it, just said I hoped it'd give us a couple of leads and maybe some contacts. I didn't want to get anyone's hopes up. Nothing has come yet from tonight's foray and there's no guarantee that there will.'

But he was going to do his best to make sure something did come from it, and so was she. They'd been an unstoppable team. Tonight, it had felt as if they couldn't fail.

'Cassidy knew about it, and I told my grandmother. So, if Ron knew, between the three of them that means the whole town will have known what we were up to.'

The furrows in his brow deepened. 'Right.'

Her stomach started to churn. 'You're not okay with this?'

'We haven't achieved anything yet!'

'But we *are* a step closer to making something happen.'

His frown didn't abate.

She turned more fully in her seat. 'What do you care about, Damon?' He blinked. 'Well, come on,' she badgered. 'Even if your list is short, there must be one or two things on it.'

'My mother. My friends.' His gaze shifted from hers to the view outside—the brightly lit bar and all the people. She didn't need to turn to know what he saw. 'I don't have a large circle of friends like you do—you can count them on one hand—but I care about them.'

It hit her then how closed off this man was. Had he always been like that? He'd never been closed off with her. She grimaced. At least, she'd never felt closed off. But she'd never known about his background, his parents. She'd never realised all he'd sacrificed in the pursuit of success.

His gaze swooped back to hers. 'I care about making *this* right.'

She didn't doubt that for a moment... '*This*, Damon—' she gestured towards the bar '—is a community. They don't just want a *fait accompli*. They want to feel a part of the journey. They want to feel they have a say in what happens.'

'But what if we disappoint them?'

What on earth...?

'And what if we don't? Look, nobody is counting chickens—everyone knows what we're trying to achieve here is a gamble—but that doesn't mean we can't celebrate small successes along the way, or the potential for big successes. It doesn't mean we can't hope. This—' she gestured to the bar pulsing with life, vitality and friendship '—builds community spirit. If things don't work out, then we'll find solace in each other. And we'll come back together with renewed vigour to find a new solution, a new way forward. So for heaven's sake, dude, lighten up.'

Her words made him blink. His frown cleared and then reappeared, but humour lit his eyes. 'So you're saying that tonight I'm...part of the community?'

She didn't hesitate. 'Yes.'

And then it hit her what his problem was, and her stomach started to churn. 'Nobody has any expectations that you're going to become a permanent fixture here, Damon, so relax. We all know that when you're done you'll be off back to Sydney and your jet-setting life.'

She pushed open her car door. He'd been here for nearly a fortnight. It would be ludicrous to think he'd be here in another fortnight. 'Look, you don't have to come in if you don't want to, but—'

He reached out and grabbed her hand. 'I'm sorry. I've tempered your enjoyment of the evening and I didn't mean to. I…it's just…it matters to me that I pull this off. I feel like I'm losing control because I care—because I've become invested.'

And he found that a challenge—that much was obvious. Her heart gave a funny thud. 'I'm not going to talk you out of feeling invested.'

'And nor should you,' he agreed. He smiled and she didn't know if he meant it or if it was just for her benefit. 'So I'm going to take your advice and go in there and enjoy it.'

He squeezed her hand. She'd forgotten he'd been holding it. She rubbed at it absently when he let it go. 'Right, well…' She pushed out of the car, feeling suddenly light-headed. 'Let's go.'

The moment they entered the bar, they were pulled into the crowd, which demanded to know what had happened at the party, if any potential developments had occurred and who'd been there. Eve didn't hold back anything. She wanted her town on board. People knew people; they could keep their ears to the ground; unforeseen serendipitous encounters and chance meetings could occur. She worked on the principle that knowledge was power. And the more people working towards the common goal of shoring up Mirror Glass Bay's future the better.

Damon followed her lead. In fact, he was so good at bringing the evening's earlier party to life that he held people spellbound as he painted a glamorous and fascinating picture.

It made her euphoric all over again.

It made everyone euphoric. Cassidy brought out the karaoke machine and demanded that Eve sing.

Eve allowed herself to be hustled onto the small platform at the end of the room to lead the town in a stirring rendition of Queen's *We are the Champions*, aware the entire time of Damon's open-mouthed shock. And the fact that his cheer was the loudest of all when the song came to an end.

'You can sing,' he said when she jumped down.

'I know!' But she said it with a laugh. 'What about you?'

He shook his head. 'I'm terrible, truly terrible.'

'What you've got to remember, Damon, is that

the trick to karaoke is that it's one's enthusiasm that counts—not whether you can hit the high notes, or any notes for that matter.'

His eyes narrowed. 'Why are you telling me this?'

'Because you're next, mate,' Ron said, clapping him on the back.

She handed him the microphone, her grin full of challenge, and he visibly swallowed. 'You want me to sing?'

'More than anything. Now, what song would you like?' She flicked through the selections. 'Madonna, Jimmy Barnes, The Rolling Stones…?'

He pointed a finger at her. 'You were warned.'

'Noted.'

'The Beatles.'

He sang *With a Little Help From My Friends* very badly but with such gusto. It had everyone clapping and joining in.

Eventually Cassidy called for last orders, and Eve took the microphone and reminded the crowd that it was the koala sanctuary working bee the following day and threatened everyone with a painful death if they didn't show up for it.

With groans, the bar cleared.

'That was fun,' Damon said, following her outside in the direction of their separate sleeping quarters. 'A lot of fun.'

He could barely get the grin off his face and

she couldn't help but grin back. 'I hate to say "I told you so".'

'I'd believe you if you didn't sound so smug.'

She just grinned.

'You have a great voice, Eve. You could've been a professional singer.'

'It wasn't a path I was ever encouraged to follow.' She shrugged. 'Besides, you need more than just a good voice. I wouldn't have made it in the profession. I never had the passion for it.'

He mulled that over for a moment. 'But you do have a passion for saving this town.'

She halted at the door that led up to her flat. 'I do.'

'Why?' he asked. 'Why does it matter so much to you?'

She pulled her wrap more tightly about her. She wasn't going to invite him in, but... 'Are you up for a walk?'

He nodded.

They strolled in the direction of the beach, not speaking, but the silence was companionable and easy and she found herself relaxing into it as she slipped her sandals off at the top of the path and dug her toes into the sand. A million stars dotted a night sky that was so clear and crisp that each of them sparkled with the clarity of a diamond. A new moon formed a perfect crescent high above them.

'Dear God,' Damon breathed, staring up at it

all. 'This has been here all this time? And I'm only just discovering it?'

'I thought you discovered it your first night here.'

'Yeah, but all this—' he gestured skyward '—here on the beach is utterly amazing.'

'I know what you mean.' She kept her gaze trained on the crescent moon. 'It's how I felt when I came back here. I'd forgotten.' She glanced at him then, saw how it all held him spellbound, and something in her stomach twisted. She had an awful feeling that he'd never known that this existed. At least, not like this.

She swallowed and forced her gaze back to the sky. 'This is why people come back year after year. Being close to this, just for a week or two, renews people's spirits. It tops them up, reminds them of what's important. It just gives them a chance to…breathe.'

She felt him turn towards her.

'And it's important to you to facilitate that?'

'It's why I've resisted turning The Beachside into some mega resort. I don't want to price my regulars out of the market. And, before you tell me what a noble sentiment that is, following that route would mean Gran and I would no longer own the motel outright—we'd need investors, would have to go into debt.' And neither one of them wanted to do that.

'I see.'

Did he? She treasured the simplicity of her life now. 'Four years ago, I found out that my parents were planning to put my grandmother into a home. They were badgering her to assign them power of attorney and enduring guardianship.'

'Could she no longer live on her own?'

'Of course she could. She still can. I mean, she needs some help every now and again, but she doesn't need to go into a home. It's just that my parents felt like she was one thing too many on their to-do list and putting her into a home was the expedient solution.'

'That's...' He looked appalled.

'Heartless,' she agreed. 'I suspect they wanted to get their hands on her house too. Gran owned a rather sweet little cottage in Balmain. It sold for a ton of money.'

'I bet. So...you and your gran did a Thelma and Louise to here?'

'We did. And we've not looked back since. This place suits her so much better than Sydney ever did. She doesn't have to catch a bus to do her groceries or to go to the doctors for her monthly vitamin B shot—it's all just a short walk away. The restaurant's kitchen delivers her a hot meal every evening. And she goes to the raffles and the bingo three to five times a week at the bowling club. Again, she can walk there. If she has a funny turn, someone will drop her home. Or they'll ring me at The Beachside and I can nip down the road to collect her. Or if I'm not here Cassidy or one of the other staff will do it.'

He was silent for a moment. 'Everyone here really does look after each other.'

'Uh-huh.'

'Does she have many funny turns?'

'No, but she's nearly eighty and none of us lives forever.'

'Your grandmother!' He spun to her so suddenly it made her feel dizzy. *He* made her feel dizzy. He pointed at her. 'She's the reason this town means so much to you.'

Was she really so transparent? The thought made her swallow. 'That's part of it,' she hedged. 'She's my family. I love her, want to see her happy. But I've made good friends here and I make a contribution—I feel like I belong. I don't want to give that up.'

She hesitated. She wasn't sure if he'd understand…

'Four years ago, I realised I was in danger of becoming exactly like my parents. When I finally recognised their priorities, I was horrified. Money and success should never matter more than people…and doing the right thing. They were so selfishly concerned with protecting and maintaining their lives that they were going to just throw my grandmother away as if she didn't matter.' Her stomach churned in outrage at the memory. 'I didn't want to be like that. So when

I look up at that night sky I'm grateful I realised that before it was too late. I'm grateful for that every single day.'

'People should always matter more than money or success.'

She knew he thought he meant those words. But she didn't think he felt them in his soul the way she did.

But he didn't have to and it was none of her business. What mattered was that he was searching for some kind of absolution and Mirror Glass Bay was reaping the benefits.

'I can be my best self here,' she said softly. 'I don't want to ever lose that again.'

'Eve, you were never in danger of becoming like your parents. *Never.* You were always a beacon…a bright light.'

He smelled of a heady mix of amber, spice and the sea. It could tangle a woman's senses if she let it. Eve reminded herself that she was her best self these days and no longer a weakling who succumbed to temptation. She was a woman who had left her old life behind, and she had no intention of ever going back.

She dismissed his words with an airy wave of her hand. 'Oh, I was clever, I'll give you that. And I knew how to make a good impression. I could make people laugh and be oh-so-charming.' She'd been charming tonight and it'd been fun. But it didn't mean she hungered for her old life.

'You were kind, Eve. You were always kind. That's what made the difference.'

Eve turned to him as he spoke and he had to suck air into his lungs at the vulnerability reflected in her eyes.

But stars were reflected there too.

She'd been kind tonight. And she wanted to write that off as a character flaw? Not on his watch! 'You were charming tonight but, Eve, your charm is kindness—it's genuine. And it brings out the best in people, lets them shine.'

'I was charming because I wanted something in return.'

He shook his head. 'You had an agenda tonight, sure, but you weren't prepared to walk over anyone to achieve it. People instinctively sense that. Anyway, parties like the one we went to tonight are deliberately tailored to bring together people whose agendas might align. There's nothing wrong with that.'

He watched her mull his words over. Her eyes were almost silver in this light, making them appear otherworldly and fey. It pushed him off-balance, and something inside his chest started to ache.

'You're a giver, Eve, not a taker like your parents.'

Her gaze lifted for a moment and it felt as if the two of them hung suspended between breaths. 'And what are you, Damon?'

She shivered in the cool night air and he immediately slipped his jacket off and laid it across her shoulders. 'I'm trying to become a giver, like you. That's what I want to be.'

She'd stilled, frozen, when he'd moved in closer with his jacket. He eased away immediately, not wanting her to feel uncomfortable with his proximity. And not wanting her to see how being this close to her affected him—had desire and need slugging through his veins with the force of a steam engine.

'Feel free to laugh at that if you want,' he added in as wry a tone as he could manage. But his voice didn't sound wry or flippant. The words emerged gruff and vulnerable, and they made him grimace.

'I don't want to laugh at it.'

He glanced back at her in time to see a flash of heat in her gaze that had his world tilting.

'Why should I laugh at your desire to be a better person?'

'I…'

A luscious, tempting smile curved her lips, though he doubted she meant it to be either luscious or tempting. And then she moved in closer to place her hand over his heart and his pulse went wild. 'That wouldn't be very kind, would it?'

He couldn't help himself. He had to touch her. Reaching up, he brushed the backs of his fingers across her cheek, her quick intake of breath finding an unequivocal answer in the tightening of his groin.

This was madness. He should step away. Kissing her would not make her happy, and he'd sworn to do only what would make her happy. But he couldn't move, couldn't stop his fingers from brushing across her cheek in a slow caress that made every atom come alive.

Under her palm, his heart pounded.

'I had a lot of fun tonight,' she whispered.

Something in her words made him frown. 'You don't often have a lot of fun?' It wasn't the picture of her life he'd drawn in his mind.

'I've found peace and satisfaction.' She leaned into his caress almost absent-mindedly. 'I have a lot of contentment, but not a lot of fun.' She moistened her lips. 'I didn't realise that until tonight. I thought what I had was enough, but...'

His mouth went dry.

Her eyes had gone dark and slumberous. She tilted her chin...almost in invitation. He swallowed and tried to cling to his sanity, his reason...

'But I'm starting to wonder if that's enough.'

'Eve, I—'

'I know you're wondering what it'd be like to kiss me now.'

His chest rose and fell. 'I don't have to wonder. I *know* it'd be sensational.'

She blinked, as if his candour surprised her. He'd sworn to himself not to lie to her again. He'd be as honest and vulnerable as she needed him to be. Even if it meant she'd stomp all over his heart.

She moved in a fraction closer. 'Well, I've been wondering all night. I can't seem to help it. Maybe it's the stars, maybe it's the tide, maybe it's the champagne.'

She'd hardly drunk any champagne.

'Maybe it's because you haven't taken advantage of the situation when I can see how much you want me.'

And, no matter how much he wanted to, he wouldn't.

She laughed—a low sound that feathered over him. 'Or maybe it's because I've held myself on too tight a leash for too long.'

She stepped in even closer until her breasts touched his chest. She was going to kiss him! Everything inside him roared to urgent, eager life. It was all he could do to stop from seizing her and devouring her like some starving beast.

Lifting up on tiptoes, she let her breath mingle with his. 'Do you have a girlfriend, Damon?'

'I haven't been with a woman since you.'

The words were wrenched from him. He hadn't meant to admit it, but in this moment he could hold nothing back.

Somehow his hands had gone to her waist and he steadied her as shock rippled through her, his fingers tightening against the softness of silk and the firmness of her flesh beneath it. Something flashed through her eyes. Passion? Definitely. And maybe possessiveness? But then she touched her lips to his and Damon lost the ability to think.

He lost the ability to hold himself back. And yet in losing himself he gained so much back in return. Eve's warmth, her ardour and her very essence surrounded him and he pulled her close to savour every delectable taste of her, grateful beyond measure for this moment, for this chance to have her in his arms again.

She'd been wondering what it would be like to kiss him so he set himself to making this a kiss that would rock her world. He concentrated his every effort on a long, slow awakening of their old desire, which it appeared hadn't diminished in the intervening years. He refused to rush— he wanted her to feel cherished. He wanted her to know how much this moment meant to him.

Her arms slid about his neck and she kissed him back with a passion that stole his breath, moved against him restlessly. With one hand he cupped her face to hold her still, wrapped his other around her waist and kissed her with all of himself—with everything he had. He kissed her thoroughly—gently, firmly, nibbling, drawing her lower lip into his mouth and lathing it with his tongue.

He loved this woman—heart and soul. His heart was hers. It was pointless denying it. For the last four years he'd been living a half-life. But he'd come alive again and he'd do anything to win Eve back—give up anything, be whatever it was that would make her happy. He poured all of that into his kiss. All of that and more.

She gasped, she moaned. A tremor shook her entire frame. Catching his face in her hands with a half-sob, she did what she always did—she gave. She kissed him with a slow intensity that had the pulse pounding in his ears and his groin straining in his pants.

The last of his restraint snapped. He slid his hands down the side of her breasts. He made lazy circles around the tight buds of her nipples with his thumbs until she cried out his name, desperation and need lacing her voice.

He loved her with his hands and his mouth, dropping to his knees at her feet, pushing up her dress and sliding aside the barrier of her panties to his questing fingers and tongue. He worshipped the texture of her skin, her scent and her very essence, savouring her unalloyed pleasure at all he was doing, taking delight in her abandon and wonder, wanting to make her feel as good as he could, give her as much delight and pleasure it was in his power to give. Her gasps and moans urged him on.

And when she came apart in his arms he gave thanks to whatever force that had brought her back into his life, because he wanted to show her that he could cherish her like this forever.

He held her close as she drifted back to reality. He felt her still as she registered what just happened. In a moment he'd tell her what a monumental impact it'd had on him. In a moment he would tell her he loved her—that he'd never stopped loving her. In a moment he would beg her to give him a second chance. Tell her he wanted to build a life with her here in Mirror Glass Bay because it was the home of her heart. And that he wanted her to have everything that would make her happy.

When she shivered, he reached down to pick up his jacket, which had fallen to the sand, and wrapped it back around her.

'Kryptonite.'

Her whispered word made no sense to him.

She pulled away, clasping the lapels of his coat tightly to her chest. 'I can't believe I just let you do that to me.'

The expression in her eyes shattered every dream he'd just dared to let himself dream.

'I can't believe…' A sob left her throat. 'I didn't even put up a fight.'

Her face had gone pinched and pale, and it

wrung his heart inside out. Bile burned the back of his throat. 'Eve, I'm sorry.' He reached out a hand to her and then swallowed when she batted it away. 'I thought it was what you wanted.'

'While you,' she continued as if he hadn't spoken, 'played the perfect gentleman and didn't take advantage of my weakness. And now you no doubt think that gives you some moral high ground.'

'I don't have any moral high ground. None,' he assured her, searching for a way to make things better, to make them right.

Her eyes flashed. 'You're darn right you don't!' And then those eyes filled with tears.

His throat thickened. 'Please, Eve. Don't cry.' How had he misread things so badly? How could he have made such a mess of things?

Darkness, betrayal, pain—they all swirled in her eyes. 'You never said sorry—not once—for what you did four years ago.'

His head snapped back. And then his stomach dropped…and his heart dropped with it, and kept right on falling.

'And you needn't think that what just happened makes a jot of difference. You're…you're just trying to make yourself feel better at my expense.'

No, he wasn't!

'You stay away from me, Damon Macy.' She reefed his jacket off and slapped it to his chest.

And with that she turned and stormed off.

You never said sorry. Not once.

He braced his hands on his knees and tried to find his centre of balance, tried to make his brain work. Tried to think of a way he could make all this up to her.

CHAPTER SEVEN

EVE SPENT THE next three days avoiding Damon. He'd walk into the bar of The Beachside and she'd walk out of it. He'd walk through the gardens and she'd walk out of them. Catching the slightest glimpse of him made her pulse pound and her body ache. It didn't matter how much she tried telling herself that what had happened on the beach was an aberration. It hadn't felt like an aberration—not then and not now. It had felt right. And that was a lie. She knew it was a lie.

Four years ago, he'd betrayed her. *For two million dollars.* How had she let herself forget that? How could she *ever* forget it?

She believed he felt bad for what he'd done, but it didn't change the fact that he was the kind of man who put a price on love. She was *never* getting involved with a man like that again.

So why on earth had she let him touch her and kiss her so intimately?

Heat flamed in her face and she seized a cloth

and wiped down the bar vigorously. What had happened on the beach on Saturday night had reminded her how good things had once been between them. But it had also brought back the devastation of his betrayal, her sense of loss—the sense that she'd never really known him when she'd thought that together they'd made more sense than anything she'd ever known.

She'd pinned all of her dreams and happiness on him—on them. Saturday night had brought back the unravelling of her sense of self in the days following his betrayal, the realisation that he'd played her for a fool and she'd been totally blind to it.

She closed her eyes, her hands clenching about the cloth. Yet on Saturday night she'd given herself to him wholeheartedly…recklessly…without a second thought. How could she have been so stupid, unguarded, forgetful?

Had she no pride?

Apparently not because when he'd stared at her as if she were the whole world a lump had lodged in her throat. It'd been so long. So long since she'd felt beautiful, desirable…like a woman. He'd kissed her as if she were his every dream come true.

And she'd been lost and so greedy for him, so hungry. That hunger still coursed through her now—and only increased whenever she saw him. Perhaps that was what frightened her most of all. Because she wasn't dancing that particular dance with him ever again. She had to find the strength to resist him.

Dragging in a breath, she scowled as she watched his car drive away from The Beachside. She *would* find that strength.

Cassidy moved to stand beside her. 'Evie, I know I probably shouldn't say anything, should keep my mouth shut, but—'

'Don't say a word, Cassidy. Just…don't.' She didn't even look at her friend as she said it, but from the corner of her eye she saw Cass raise her hands in a gesture of appeasement.

'You're the boss.'

Her chest clenched and she swung to her friend. 'I didn't mean it like that.'

'I know, hon.' Cassidy's blue eyes were filled with concern. 'But you've gone so quiet…and everyone is starting to get worried.'

And Cassidy was bearing the brunt of everyone's concern and curiosity—no doubt fielding questions and doing what she could to deflect attention from Eve's sudden withdrawal.

Damn.

She had to get over herself and move on. It was selfish to wallow in all…this. But she had no idea how she was going to face Damon, let alone look him in the eye. The very thought made her want to die a thousand deaths.

Tonight, they were going to dinner at the

Sorensons. She had to pull herself together before then.

'You know I'm here, Evie. If you need to talk or…for anything.'

'I do and it means a lot.' She loved these people and they loved her. Four years ago, they had helped her find her centre again. That centre was still there, even if the events of Saturday night had left her feeling flung off-course. That thought helped to steady her. She forced her spine to straighten. She even found a sort of smile. 'Hey, have you seen Dolly in the last few days?'

Cassidy rolled her eyes. 'Looks like she's still as besotted with Damon as ever.' She leaned in closer. 'But I just saw him go out. I also happen to know for a fact that housekeeping will be doing the rooms in that part of the motel right about now. Perhaps you need to go and supervise?'

She stretched her neck to the right and to the left. She hadn't clapped eyes on Dolly in days.

Cassidy bumped shoulders with her. 'Go and cuddle your cat, Eve.'

Eve didn't need any further encouragement.

Damon's room had already been cleaned and the housekeeping staff had moved to the one other room currently occupied on this floor, but the doors to all of the rooms stood wide open to embrace the fresh air and sunshine.

Dolores lay curled up in the middle of Damon's bed. Eve moved to lie beside her. 'You old reprobate.' She stroked her fingers through soft fur. 'You've changed allegiances, huh?'

Dolly immediately stood and smothered Eve with affection. She batted her head against Eve's chin and hand, purring and giving funny little half-meows, rolling against Eve's chest and tummy, falling onto her back to bat Eve's hand with her paws. It made Eve smile. It made the sun shine a little brighter.

'You're a disgrace to the cat world, Dolores, you know that? You have the soul of puppy.'

'I tell her that too.'

Eve froze. *Dear God.* She was utterly incapable of moving a muscle, except her eyes. And they confirmed what her senses already knew—Damon stood in the doorway.

'I… I just wanted to cuddle my cat,' she whispered.

'Totally understandable.'

She was lying on his bed like some kind of invitation, having deliberately snuck in here when he was out. She should be mortified. And yet the warmth in his eyes told her he understood, that he didn't mind, saving her from the worst of her embarrassment. And it nearly undid her.

'I didn't mean to disturb you. I forgot my phone and wallet. Mirror Glass Bay is obviously making me too relaxed.'

And now he was apologising to her!

He hadn't moved from the doorway and she forced uncooperative limbs to shuffle her to the side of the bed where she stood on legs that felt like jelly. 'I'm sorry. I shouldn't have disturbed your room.'

'Except I seem to have commandeered your cat. And it's your motel, Eve. You have the right to disturb this room any time you like.'

She focused on his first sentence rather than the latter with all its accompanying disturbing images. 'I suspect it's more accurate to say Dolores has commandeered you.'

His mouth twitched. 'She's still enough of a cat to believe she deserves accommodation in the best room in the house.'

That almost made her smile. 'Right. Well... sorry again. And now I really should get back to work.'

'Can I have a word before you go? If you have the time.'

If she made some excuse he wouldn't try to stop her—he wouldn't argue. She could see that in his face. He was also doing his best not to look physically intimidating—slouching rather than looming, ducking his head, keeping a pleasant smile on his face.

She almost made that excuse anyway. But then she remembered Cassidy, her grandmother and the rest of the town—knew how closely everyone was watching her. So, instead of fleeing, she made herself shrug. 'Sure, but can we move the conversation into the living area?'

She was too aware of the king-sized bed. Too aware of everything she shouldn't be.

Without a word he turned and she followed, but the sight of a bright-pink litter tray in his bathroom pulled her up short. 'You bought a litter tray?'

'I… It seemed like a good idea.'

She stared at him, mouth agape. She stared at the tray. He'd bought her cat *a litter tray*? That it had even occurred to him…

Close your mouth, Eve.

'Um…thank you. That was very kind of you.'

He waved that away. 'It's my own fault. If I don't have the heart to put her out then I have to make sure accidents aren't going to happen in the room.'

'For which I'm grateful.' She dusted off her hands and hoped she looked businesslike 'Now, you wanted a word?'

'About what happened on the beach—'

'*No!*' Her vehemence startled them both. She dragged both hands down her face and pulled in a breath. 'Look, Damon, I *really* don't want to talk about it. What happened was a mistake. I was stupid and reckless, and I can promise it won't happen again.'

He'd gone still, his eyes throbbing, and she had to look away.

'Can we pretend it never happened? Please?'

She closed her eyes, mortified at how pleading her *'Please,'* sounded.

'If that's what you want,' he finally said.

'Oh, it is. It really is.' But when she turned back to face him she could tell that somehow she'd hurt him, and she had to roll her shoulders against a growing sense of guilt.

'Okay...' He pulled in a breath then and let it out, as if he were trying to release something. 'Right, it's clear you've been avoiding me for the last three days.'

She didn't bother denying it. She'd look like an idiot if she did.

'But I want to assure you that you've nothing to fear from me. I'm not going to push my attentions on you—I won't try to kiss you again. I don't expect anything from you. I swear I'll abide by the boundaries you're setting. You won't have to tell me again. I don't force myself on unwilling women.'

It wasn't him she was worried about, but her own deplorable lack of unwillingness. Saturday night had shown her precisely how willing she was where this man was concerned. Not that she had any intention of confiding as much. She couldn't give Damon any kind of power over her again.

'I just wanted you to know that.'

She eyed him uncertainly. He didn't look as if he'd slept in the last three days. She did what she could to harden her heart. 'Thank you.' Was that it? She edged towards the door, before she weakened and asked if he was all right.

'There's one more thing.'

He widened his stance and her pulse went berserk. *Kryptonite.* She held herself tight. 'Yes?'

'You said that four years ago I didn't apologise, Eve. I—'

'No.' She cut him off, waving both hands in front of her face, wanting desperately to dismiss all mention of their past and the memory of how much he'd hurt her—how much he might still be able to hurt her if she let him. 'I don't want to talk about our past. I don't want to talk about what happened four years ago. Bringing it up now will only make working with you more difficult.'

He paled. And for some reason his words on the beach came back to her now. *I haven't been with a woman since you.* She didn't know if that was true or not, but she couldn't let herself care.

She drew in a breath and let it out, trying to tame the way her heart raced. 'Damon, all I want is to focus on the here and now and do what I can to ensure Mirror Glass Bay's future. That's all.'

He pinched the bridge of his nose as if he had

a raging headache and she had to stop herself, again, from asking if he was all right.

'You and I are only going to focus on the practical. Not the emotional—that's too fraught. I know you started this whole crusade to make amends—to make yourself feel better—but it's not fair to ask me to provide you with absolution or—'

'You're right.'

He sounded sick and for a moment she hated herself. But…he was her kryptonite—Cassidy was right—and she couldn't reveal any weakness around him. It'd taken her too long to get over him. It wasn't that she didn't want him to find the peace he was searching for or that she didn't applaud his desire to become a better person.

It was just…she wasn't going to help him gain his peace at the expense of losing her own. Kissing him, letting him touch her so intimately, had been a crazy mistake, but at least it had brought home to her, with a clarity that still shocked her, her weakness for this man.

She'd work with him because she wanted her town to benefit from his contacts, his money and his know-how. But she couldn't get close to him emotionally. Not again. They didn't have a future together. They had…nothing.

She glanced at him again. 'If that's all…?'

Before her eyes, he transformed. He shook himself and became businesslike and efficient. 'Three practical things.'

She couldn't explain why but she didn't feel relieved or comforted.

'The first—are we still on for the Sorensen dinner tonight?'

'Absolutely. I'll drive this time.' She wanted no hint of this being a date. She wanted an excuse to stay away from the champagne too. Not that she blamed champagne for what had happened Saturday night, but she wasn't giving her defences any opportunity to weaken. 'Shall we leave at six-thirty?'

He nodded his agreement. 'The second—last Sunday Pru helped me choose a surfboard for the raffle fundraiser.'

He'd got the younger girl's input. That was nice of him.

'And I have raffle books.'

'Oh!' Of course, he did. 'Right, I'll take at least ten books, and we'll keep one on the bar and another in Reception. Actually, give a stack to Cassidy. She'll distribute them to any townsfolk who pop in for a coffee or a beer. Excellent, that's great, Damon. Thank you.

'And the third thing?' she prompted when he remained silent.

'Barbara Dalton contacted me about the dog shelter, so I spoke to Pru's mum, floated the idea of Pru becoming a foster carer, and she thought it was a good idea.'

'I'm so glad.'

He stared at her carefully. 'But Pru needs to attend a training session a week Saturday.'

'But her mum works Saturdays.'

'I offered to take her, of course, but she doesn't know me well enough to entrust her twelve-year-old daughter to my care.'

Her stomach clenched at the question she could see coming.

'But she said it'd be okay if you made up one of the party.'

How could she refuse? She'd been searching for months to find a way to help the younger girl. And, seriously, where was the harm? It wasn't as if she'd be spending the time with Damon on her own—Pru would be with them the entire time. Nothing could happen... Plus, dogs. She'd get to spend a few hours playing with dogs.

She nodded. 'Okay, count me in.'

The Beachside's café-bar-restaurant was roughly divided into two sections. The three-sided bar was located in the middle of a long rectangle of a room. To the left was the café and informal eating area, to the right was the restaurant, though Damon had noticed a lot of overlap on Friday and Saturday nights. The Beachside didn't stick to rigid and clear rules about who could sit where, and he could see the clientele loved the establishment all the more for its democratic attitude.

He didn't sit in cafés in Sydney, idly read the paper and sip a leisurely coffee, certainly not at ten-thirty on a Thursday morning, but here in Mirror Glass Bay it seemed the natural thing to do. Not to take the time to appreciate the coffee Cassidy served him would feel wrong—rude somehow.

And sitting here like this felt…freeing.

Which was making him realise how rigid his own life had become.

He glanced up from the paper when the other chair at his table was pulled out and an older woman seated herself there. 'Damon Macy, I believe?'

'That's right.'

Behind her he saw Cassidy halt in her clearing of a nearby table and bite her lip. But when she noticed him watching her gaze turned mocking and she turned away again with a shrug.

'And you are…?' he asked. By now he was used to the residents of Mirror Glass Bay introducing themselves and telling him how great their town was, making suggestions in relation to his building site.

'*You're* the man they're calling the town saviour.'

He shifted, fighting back a frown. 'That's not how I'd put it.'

'No, nor would I.'

She didn't smile. No humour lit her eyes or

face. She stared at him as if he were a bug that she'd like to squash beneath her shoe. He stiffened. Who on earth was she? Was she an environmentalist who thought all he was interested in was raping and pillaging the land? Was she...?

And then he realised *exactly* who she was. She might not look like her granddaughter, but she was one of only two people in Mirror Glass Bay, besides Eve, who had any reason to loathe him. 'You're Eve's grandmother. She told me how the two of you came here and made Mirror Glass Bay your home. I'm pleased to meet you.' He held out his hand, but she ignored it.

'Bethany Ford,' she clipped out. 'So *you're* the two-million-dollar gigolo.'

He choked. *What* had she just called him?

'Ah, I can see you don't like that, but what else would you call yourself, Mr Macy? My granddaughter slept with you and it cost her two million dollars.' She shook her head. 'You're a good-looking man, but you're not worth two million dollars.'

She rose. 'Can I make a suggestion?'

He couldn't make his voice work. He couldn't even nod or shake his head.

'It'd be greatly appreciated if you didn't stay in Mirror Glass Bay longer than necessary. You might have the rest of the town fooled, but you and I both know the truth—you don't belong in a place like this. We both know you're not good enough for a woman like Eve.'

She left and everything inside him ached. He couldn't recall a lower point in his life—and he'd had a few. An elderly woman had just called him a gigolo…and she had every reason to do so.

Bitterness filled his mouth. She was wrong, though. He hadn't sold his body. He'd sold his soul. If he'd only sold his body, he might still be able to find redemption.

Cassidy's face broke into his field of vision, consternation in her eyes and something that might've been sympathy. 'Eve has been trying to keep Granny Beth away from you.'

He stared at the piece of carrot cake she set in front of him and shook his head. 'I—'

'Eat it. It'll make you feel better.'

And then she was gone, so he did. And at least, after he'd finished it, he didn't feel any worse.

While the Sorensen dinner on Wednesday night had gone exceptionally well, and he had business meetings set up with both Simon Sorensen and Garry Dalton, Eve still continued to avoid him over the following week. Damon did what he could to keep busy. He sent instructions to his office to send him a lawyer and an administrative assistant. He hired temporary office space and living quarters for them in Byron Bay. He spoke to Owen who, amazingly enough, was still in Frankfurt and slowly making inroads on the deal with Herr Mueller. But none of that could stop his mind from returning to Eve.

She didn't avoid him with the same assiduity as she had the previous week—whenever she did see him, she sent him a cheery wave, and might exchange a few words, but she was always on her way somewhere to do something…

His hands clenched. Why on earth would she want to spend any time with a two-million-dollar gigolo?

You never said sorry.

He flinched. As he did every single time Eve's words replayed themselves through his mind— which they did with startling frequency. At least that was something he could rectify.

At seven o'clock on Friday morning he took a brand-new surfboard he'd bought the previous day and paddled out into the surf—not directly towards Eve, but nearby—and tried to catch a wave. Pru had given him some preliminary instructions and he'd watched a couple of 'how to' videos on the Internet.

It was a whole lot harder than anyone had made it look. He gritted his teeth as he fell off the board for the umpteenth time, all but face planting into salt water and sand. He was starting to hurt. He suspected that tomorrow he'd discover muscles he'd never known he had.

'What are you doing?'

He glanced up to find Eve sitting on her board nearby, perfectly at ease on the treacherous, shifting water. He scowled. 'I thought I'd give surfing a go. I watched some videos—surfing basics.'

She folded her arms but still stayed on her surfboard without falling off. 'And those videos told you to leap straight to trying to stand on your board in chest-high water, did they?'

He grabbed the surfboard as a wave tried to tug it free. 'Well, no. They said to catch small waves on your knees in the shallows first, but…'

Her eyebrows rose. 'But you think you're so good you can skip ahead a few steps?'

In a word—yes! He kept himself fit.

But apparently he wasn't fit for surfing.

With a laugh she headed back out again. He watched her catch a perfect wave, switching back and doing some fancy turn that had him shaking his head.

Right. He patted his board. They'd take it back to basics, then.

He didn't know how long he practised but eventually he managed to travel a few metres on his knees before falling off. Then, and only then, did he turn his board in Eve's direction.

'You look like you were making some progress,' she said.

He tried to sit on his board with the same ease and grace that she did. He doubted he managed it, but he did finally find himself sitting on the board. The swell of the sea moving beneath him felt oddly soothing. 'I'm crap.'

'We're all crap in the early days.' She sent him a sidelong glance, her brow furrowing. 'You want to tell me what you're really up to?'

He didn't understand the sudden anger that ballooned in his chest. 'You want to see me hurt and humiliated. And I want to make you happy.' He gestured at his board. 'Two birds, one stone.'

Her lips pursed. 'So…this is about my grandmother and whatever it was she said to you yesterday? Cassidy told me about it.'

He should've known she'd hear about that. 'What did Cassidy say?'

'I think the words she used were "shell-shocked" and "shattered".'

He winced. 'She brought me a slice of carrot cake after your gran left.'

Eve's eyebrows lifted before she smoothed her face out again. 'Granny Beth has a remarkable ability to make one feel the size of a pea when the mood takes her, and—'

'Eve, she didn't say anything to me that I didn't deserve. She held a mirror up and I didn't like what I saw. That's all.'

She gestured to his board. 'So now you want to punish yourself?'

'In part, probably. So far it's not working.' He didn't feel the slightest bit better for the beating he'd so far taken in the surf. 'But I live in hope. The other part...'

Her eyes widened like a startled deer's. 'The other part?'

'Out here I can talk to you alone without anyone overhearing.' She made as if to lie down on her board and paddle back to shore. 'In an environment where you're at home and comfortable and where I'm not.'

She stilled and then sat upright again.

'Out here I'm hoping you don't feel intimidated by me... Out here I'm hoping you feel you have the advantage.'

Her eyes flashed. 'I don't feel intimidated by you at all—out here or on dry land.'

'So you're saying you haven't been avoiding me?'

Her gaze moved from his to scan the shore. 'I run my own business, in case you forgot. There are demands on my time, things I need to do.'

'I understand that, which is why I'm making the effort to meet with you at a time that's convenient to you and on your terms.'

'If you want to discuss any of the local development opportunities or the fundraiser, you only need to say. I'll make the time.'

'And what if I want to talk to you about something that's not business?'

'Like what?' She stared at him as if they couldn't possibly have anything other than business to discuss. Her face cleared. 'Oh, you mean Pru. Has something happened? Are we no longer going to the dog shelter next Saturday?'

'I could send that kind of information to you in a text, or wait till you'd returned to shore. I didn't need to go to this effort, let the sea use me as its punching bag, to tell you that.'

'Punching bag?' She snorted. 'You big baby— that's nothing. You've been playing in the little pool.'

Would she feel more kindly towards him if a monster wave dumped him? 'Here's the thing, Eve. I made you a promise to not bring up the past, and I'm not going to break any promise I make to you. Not in the here and now. But that doesn't mean you can't raise the past with me. And I mean to be here in case you ever decide to do that.'

'Not going to happen. And here's a tip, Damon. You're fighting the sea's power when you should be harnessing it. I'm harnessing your power for the greater good of Mirror Glass Bay and that's all I need from you. End of story.'

And with that she lay flat on her board, paddled onto a wave and caught it all the way back to shore. She didn't turn and wave to him. She didn't turn and look back once.

He'd known this wasn't going to be easy. But the only way he could think of to tell her how sorry he was for all that had happened between them was to continue to show up. And he planned to keep doing exactly that.

She'd said she didn't need anything from him. But she needed to hear his apology. The expression in her eyes after their encounter on the beach that night... Bile burned his stomach. When he'd broken her heart, he'd broken her belief in herself—her belief in her judgement and in her ability to read people. She needed to know that he hadn't deliberately played her false or for a fool. She needed to know that he hadn't deliberately, coldly and ruthlessly made her fall in love with him just so he could gain an advantage over her.

She needed to hear the truth. It wouldn't change anything between them, but it might bolster her belief in herself again. And he owed her that.

Damon surfed every morning for the following week. Sometimes he was there before Eve, sometimes after. He always waved to her and she always waved back. Most days, once he was worn out from trying to master the skills he needed to, he'd paddle out the back to where she was and just sit there. Not talking. Not asking anything of her. Just being present.

One week to the day that he'd started showing up, she swung on him. 'Fine, Damon, tell me what this is all about. What is it from the past that you want to tell me?'

His every muscle stiffened. He dragged in a breath over the pounding of his heart. 'Sorry.'

'You got water in your ears? I said—'

'I'm not asking you to repeat yourself, Eve. I want to say I'm sorry for what I did four years ago. I wanted to apologise then, but you were so angry and said you never wanted to see me again—and I didn't blame you, not in the slightest. And then you left. Without a word.'

He'd known she'd leave him after he'd destroyed everything. He just hadn't realised she'd leave everything else too—the promising career she'd created for herself, the city he'd thought she loved and her family. He'd understood then exactly how badly he'd hurt her. 'I hated myself so much for what I'd done that afterwards I didn't try to find you, and I never told you how sorry I was. I just slunk away like a coward.'

Two million dollars richer.

She paled at his words, but her chin didn't drop. 'What exactly are you apologising for?'

The breath he pulled in hurt his lungs. 'I'm sorry I betrayed your trust and stole your client. I only won the grant because I managed to score the Otto Farnham account. I deliberately used the insider knowledge I'd gained from you to woo him and steal him out from beneath you.'

Inside information she'd given him when they'd been in bed together—both of them physically replete from their love-making but not yet ready to sleep because they'd wanted to continue revelling in each other for a little longer. It had felt like their own little world, precious and fragile, and he'd treasured it. It was where Eve had shared her hopes and dreams with him, transporting him and giving him a picture of a life he'd never thought possible for himself. It was also where she'd shared her worries and concerns—including work problems and difficulties.

He'd been honoured by her confidences. While their company had positioned the two of them as business rivals, pitting them against each other to win particular accounts, she'd trusted him. They'd both known that the powers that be at Spellman and Spelman were watching them, wondering which of them to fast-track, to whom to offer a junior partnership first…and to which of them to award their prestigious industry grant.

That grant had guaranteed the winner a place within the company's hierarchy—a recognition of excellence. It had guaranteed career success, financial security and a place at the top. They'd both been hungry for that. But she'd trusted him enough to share her difficulties at work and to ask his advice. And he'd done the same, knowing she'd never betray him.

He'd never meant to be anything but supportive. He'd never expected…

He'd loved her! *Her* triumphs and successes had felt like *his* triumphs and successes. And she'd been *so* close to closing that deal with Otto. He'd been holding his breath for her.

And then…behind her back he'd wooed Otto himself—using everything he knew about the man and his insecurities to give himself the edge. He'd betrayed her. All so he could win that damn grant.

'I knew how many months and how many hours you'd put into winning Otto's trust. I knew you were battling old-fashioned sexism and prejudice.' Otto was old-school, believing men were better at finance than women. The inroads Eve had made and the fact she'd nearly won him over did her credit. 'So I used that to my advantage.' And he'd thrown everything he'd had into winning the other man's trust, playing on his belief that only a man could do such a job properly.

'Wow.' She paled. 'So…no pussyfooting around about what you did, then.' Cupping her hands, she scooped up seawater and splashed it over her face.

'I can't pretty any of it up. I was completely ruthless.' He forced himself to continue. 'Did you know that Otto thought you and Clay were still engaged?'

Clay Spelman was the son of one of Spellman and Spelman's senior partners, and Eve had been engaged to him for six months before Damon had met her. And for two months after. They'd all become friends—these days Clay was Damon's best friend.

It was only after Eve and Damon had become lovers that she'd told him she and Clay had basically fallen into their engagement—a path of least resistance, a mutually easy arrangement encouraged by their families. On paper, they'd seemed perfect.

She'd said she'd broken off the engagement because of her attraction to Damon—the strength of her desire for him had made her realise what was missing from Clay's and her relationship. It'd made her realise that she wanted more—that both she and Clay deserved more.

'I did wonder,' she finally said now. 'I didn't deliberately keep the truth from him, but I also knew if he thought I was that closely allied to the Spelmans it'd be a tick in my favour.' She glanced at him. 'I take it you disabused him of the notion.'

He nodded.

Her nostrils flared, and she shook her head, as if she still couldn't believe what he'd done.

Damon swallowed the hardness that did its best to lodge in his throat. It settled in his chest like a stone. 'I knew the board's decision about whom to award the grant to was drawing closer. When Mr Spelman asked me if there was any reason why he should award me the grant over you, I knew they'd chosen you as the grant's recipient.'

Her eyes throbbed. But she didn't utter a word.

'So I asked him…' It was hard to push the words out. 'I asked him what would happen if I handed him the Otto Farnham account by the end of the day—all signed, sealed and delivered.'

She flinched.

'He said if I did that then the grant was all mine.'

She refused to look at him and he wanted to throw his head back and howl. 'I'm sorry I did that to you, Eve. I've regretted it every single day since.'

She tossed her head and swung back to glare at him. 'Really? So if you could turn the clock back you'd do things differently?

Would he? He dragged a hand down his face. She laughed—a harsh, ragged sound—and made to paddle away.

'Wait!' Panic rose through him at the remote expression on her face. 'I want you to know that I didn't plan it. I didn't set out to make you fall in love with me to take advantage of you or the situation.'

Eyes the colour of sodden seaweed met his and his mouth went dry. 'I loved you, Eve. I broke my own heart that day too.'

But he could see she didn't believe him. 'You chose the two million dollars, though, Damon.

You didn't choose me. You'll have to excuse me if I don't have any faith in your version of love.'

'If I tell you why I did it, though, you might—'

'Nope. Not interested.'

And then she was on a wave, moving away from him, looking free, lovely and utterly beyond his reach.

CHAPTER EIGHT

Pru chatted all the way from Mirror Glass Bay to the Byron Bay Dog Rescue Centre, for which Eve gave thanks, because it took her the full thirty-minute drive to force every cell from focussing wholly on Damon. His apology the previous day had messed with her head—blown all her concentration—and she'd barely been able to think of anything else since.

She'd checked in customers, spoken to her bookkeeper, had lunched with her grandmother and had pulled beers in the bar—but it had all been by rote. Her mind had been elsewhere.

Ever since that apology she'd been in turmoil. It made no sense—his apology shouldn't change anything. But his stark recitation of what he'd done four years ago hadn't soothed her at all—it'd brought all the pain, confusion and disbelief rushing back.

And then he'd told her how sorry he was and there'd been no mistaking the sincerity in his eyes. But it hadn't drawn a line beneath those long-ago events, as it should've done. Instead of easing the burning in her chest it had increased it tenfold, and she wanted to throw her head back and scream.

And then he'd had the affront to show up on his surfboard again this morning—getting knocked off wave after wave, time and time again, but gritting his teeth and getting back on that damn board.

It was enough to make anyone scream.

Even more infuriatingly, he hadn't come near her. He hadn't tried to pick up the thread of yesterday's conversation, hadn't tried to force his point of view or interpretation onto her—as he'd promised he wouldn't. He was letting her set the pace. He was letting her choose what she wanted to know and what she didn't want to know.

She folded her arms and glared doggedly out of the window, sticking out her chin. It wasn't going to happen. There was no pace to set because *they* weren't going anywhere. She felt him glance briefly at her, but she didn't return it. The *why* of what he'd done four years ago didn't matter. All that mattered was that he'd chosen that two-million-dollar grant over her, and he'd done it in the most brutal fashion possible. That was all she needed to know.

'And there's even a mother dog with five puppies,' Pru was saying from the back seat. 'That'd

be like fostering six dogs for the price of one—
how cool would that be?'

She forced her mind from thoughts of the man
sitting beside her and to the twelve-year-old in
the back seat. 'Five puppies could be fun, but
that's an awful lot of toilet training.'

Pru giggled. 'Yeah, it could get messy.'

'Six dogs would need a lot of exercise too,
don't you think? And a big yard.'

Pru's yard was large, but only a tiny portion
of it had a dog-proof fence.

'Uncle Ron and his team are putting a brand-
new fence up—for free. Well,' she countered a
moment later, 'for ANZAC biscuits. I have to
bake them ANZAC biscuits every week for the
next month. They wanted to do something good
for the dog shelter. Ron wants to check out the
dogs I foster and have first dibs on one for his
family.'

Ron was...? She glanced at Damon. She'd bet
he'd set that up. His answering glance gave nothing away but it had her pulse chugging all the
same. She turned in her seat more fully to look
at Pru. 'Won't you find it hard to give them up to
their forever homes when someone adopts them?'

'Mrs Dalton talked to me about that. She said
that finding foster carers for the dogs was really
important—it means the pound doesn't have to
put them down. That's a really big thing, don't
you think?'

'Huge.'

'So, I'll miss the dogs when they get a home for real, but there's always going to be more dogs who need fostering. This way I'll get to know lots and lots of dogs, and that'll feel like I have lots and lots of friends in the world.'

'Oh, Pru, what a gorgeous thought. And it's true. What you're doing is such a good thing.'

Pru's chin lifted and she beamed back. 'I'm doing something for the greater good.'

The younger girl's words made Eve's chest burn. She turned back to the front and swallowed down the lump that lodged in her throat. It settled in her chest, a hard and heavy weight. Pru was doing something for the greater good. So was Damon. While she...

While she was holding on to a four-year-old grudge. Tightly. With both hands. As if it were a life buoy. Wasn't it time to let it go?

She had no idea. And then they were at the dog shelter and she looked forward to putting it all out of her mind for a couple of hours while she played with the shelter dogs. A yard full of fun, playful, rowdy dogs—it was exactly what she needed.

When they entered the office, not only did they find Barbara Dalton, waiting to take Pru through for the foster-care training, but Valerie Sorensen too. 'Simon and I planned to surprise you,' she said. 'We wanted to treat you to a couple of hours on the boat.'

'Boat?' Barbara snorted. 'This thing is like a palace with a hull and sails.'

'Simon is rather proud of it.' Valerie rolled her eyes. 'I suspect he thinks you're in the market for one, Damon.'

'He could be right.'

No, no. Eve glanced from one to the other. She wanted dogs and noise…time *away* from Damon.

'But Simon has been called away on business.'

She let out a relieved breath. Very quietly. She wouldn't offend the Sorensens for the world—and not just because of the business negotiations currently underway, but because she genuinely liked them. They were nice people. So were the Daltons. That said, negotiations were still at a delicate stage. Offending them could prove fatal to Mirror Glass Bay's hopes.

'Never mind,' she said brightly. 'Maybe some other time. We understand he's a busy man. But it was really lovely of you both to think of such a thing.'

'Oh, no,' Valerie said. 'We haven't cancelled the treat. Everything has been arranged. We've organised a jaunt just for the two of you. Just for a few hours—but I made sure to order you lunch and champagne.'

She beamed at the two of them. Somehow—

just—Eve managed to beam back. 'Wow! It sounds amazing.'

'And Barbara has spoken to Pru's mother, and she's fine with the two of you leaving Pru to her care for a couple of hours.'

Eve's mind whirled, trying to find a way out. 'Honestly, though, Valerie, that's much too generous. We couldn't possibly trespass on your goodwill like that.'

Shadows chased themselves through Damon's eyes when she met them, but he took his lead from her. 'And I'm sure Simon would much rather be there to point out all the yacht's features and answer all of my questions.'

'We'll organise another jaunt for the four—or the six of us,' she added, swinging back to Barbara.

Damon glanced at her and Eve gave a tiny shake of her head. They'd have to submit or risk alienating the Sorensens…and that was something they couldn't afford to do. 'It sounds wonderful.' She pasted on her brightest smile. 'But… you are going to join us, aren't you?'

'No, no! The two of you go and have a lovely time.'

'We're going to be busy anyway,' Barbara said.

Eve couldn't help herself. 'You do know that Damon and I are just friends—there'd be no third-wheel thing happening if you did join us.'

The other woman leaned across and patted her hand. 'Of course—whatever you say, dear.'

She didn't believe her! Which left Eve with nothing to say.

Half an hour later, she and Damon were sailing the placid waters off the Byron Bay main beach in the kind of luxury she'd had only ever dreamed about.

And she couldn't enjoy any of it because she was supposedly enjoying 'couple time' with Damon—the last man on earth with whom she wanted to spend couple time.

'I'm sorry,' he murmured as he came to stand beside her at the yacht's railing. 'I know you'd rather be anywhere but here. If I'd realised what they had planned, I'd have found a way to get out of it.'

'It doesn't matter. It wasn't worth making a fuss over. Look.' She gestured. 'Isn't the view spectacular?'

He frowned. 'It really is.'

Since he'd been grounded in Mirror Glass Bay, he'd been forced to stop and smell the roses. The combination of bewilderment, awe and pleasure that flitted across his face did things to her insides. It reminded her of their shocking intimacy on the beach that night—how his kisses and caresses had set her free. It reminded her of what it had been like to spend long afternoons making love with him. She missed it so much it hurt.

'Oh, and look!' She pointed. 'They've organised some dolphins as well.'

His surprise, and then his delight, tugged at her, daring her to throw away both her resentment and her caution. He moved to the bow to watch them frolic in the waves caused by the yacht as it ploughed through the water. 'That almost makes it worth it.'

She blinked. Didn't he want to be here with her either? She had to fight the sudden urge to jump overboard and swim for land.

He turned back to her with a self-conscious grin. 'I was really looking forward to playing with puppies.'

Something in her chest eased. 'Me too.'

His eyes narrowed as he studied her face and he straightened. She sensed he was about to say something awkward and hard, and panic gathered beneath her breastbone.

As if sensing her resistance and trepidation, he eased back, but she'd have had to be blind to miss the hurt that flashed through those warm brown eyes.

That wasn't her fault.

But it felt like her fault.

'Did you know that this yacht is forty-five metres of unrivalled luxury?' He started talking dimensions and engine sizes and she could've hugged him.

They talked about the yacht, the scenery and

the view until they'd exhausted all those topics and had nothing left to say. So they settled to touring the yacht's layout below deck. The luxury took her breath away but couldn't divert her attention from Damon and his broad shoulders and lean length—the same clean, broad lines she did her best not to notice every morning while he tried to teach himself how to surf. The master bedroom—apparently called a stateroom—had her tongue cleaving to the roof of her mouth and temptation coiling through her.

Damon didn't look at her.

And she knew. She knew he was remembering what it had once been like between them. He was remembering what they'd once have done with a couple of hours like this. He was wondering what it would be like if they closed that door and tossed all caution to the wind.

And so was she.

She stared at the enormous bed and swallowed, every cell on the surface of her skin becoming more and more sensitised until her mouth dried with need and temptation.

When she glanced across she found Damon's gaze on her—hot, heavy and filled with the same passion she remembered from four years ago. Before Damon, love-making had been pleasant. But making love *with* him had been a revelation. She hadn't known that such pleasure existed— pleasure that could make her pant and beg and lose herself. She'd not understood the irresistible urge to make someone lose control, or the freedom in losing control herself. Until Damon.

She couldn't look away.

She didn't want to look away.

She wasn't sure who moved towards the other first. She was only aware of the elation that filled her soul when Damon closed the gap between them and lifted his hand to her cheek. She nuzzled it, closing her eyes as she dragged in a breath of his skin.

'Eve.'

Her name was a breath, a whisper…a question. And, when his lips descended to hers, her parted lips answered it with a hunger and need she could no longer deny.

His greed matched hers. He slammed the door shut and then hauled her so close she could feel his every muscle moving beneath the softness of her curves. He kissed her with a wild abandon, as if he'd been holding himself on too tight a leash and could no longer contain himself. And something inside her sang at his wildness, sang at the knowledge she could still drive him insane with need.

'I need to taste you.' She didn't recognise the growl that emerged from her throat and she didn't stop to care. She hauled his shirt over his head, pressed her lips to the spot where his neck met his shoulder and licked him, wanting to weep at the familiar scents and tastes that assailed her. How had she lived without this?

She raked her fingers down his chest, her lips following to find one hard, flat male nipple. She circled it with her tongue, groaning in approval when it hardened as she drew it into her mouth and scraped it gently with her teeth.

Damon swore, and she suddenly found herself upright again and with her shirt pulled over her head, her arms bound and tangled in the cotton. His grin grew wolfish as he stared down at her, making her heart beat like a tattoo in her throat. Swiping the lace of her bra aside, he drew one nipple into his mouth and suckled hard. Her cry sounded about the cabin as she arched into him, and she'd have fallen if he hadn't swept an arm about her waist. She trembled from the soles of her feet to her fingernails as he lathed and plea-sured her breasts with a thoroughness that had need roaring in her ears.

With another growl she wrestled her T-shirt over her head, her hands going straight to the belt buckle at Damon's waist. She needed this man inside her now! And she wasn't going to be denied...

A knock on the door had Damon stiffening. Eve ignored it.

'Ms Clark and Mr Macy,' a steward called out from the other side. 'When you're ready, your lunch has been served on the main deck.'

'We'll be right there,' Damon called back,

Not if she had any say in it. She pressed kisses to his jaw, letting her mouth rove down his throat, her fingers busy at his belt, while he sucked in great breaths of air. She wanted to drive him wild again, to the edge of all reason.

She scrabbled for purchase as he put her away from him. Very gently he eased her bra back into place, and she blinked. He picked up her T-shirt from the floor and handed it to her, not meeting her eyes. 'I'm sorry, Eve, I lost control.'

She swallowed. 'I…um…you weren't the only one.' She frowned. They were adults. They could…

Her heart sank at the expression in his eyes. Apparently, they couldn't. She did what she could to hide the disappointment that stretched through her.

His lips pressed into a grim line. 'I promised not to kiss you again.' He hauled his shirt on over his head and covered up that glorious naked chest.

Her heart thumped in protest.

'I am truly sorry.'

He was sorry? He was apologising? Did he wish he hadn't kissed her?

Swallowing, she tried to slam herself back into her shirt, her arm getting caught in the process, and she had to tolerate the supreme indignity of

Damon coming to her aid before she strangled herself.

'You hated me for what I did that night on the beach. And I can't repeat that. I…'

She closed her eyes.

Dear God, what had she been thinking?

She hadn't been thinking.

'And I made you a promise.' He swore. 'I lost my head and—'

'Let's forget it, Damon,' she cut in, everything inside her hurting, though she couldn't explain why. Other than the fact that she ached for him, for the release she knew he could bring her.

Oh, but it'd be too foolhardy, because making love with Damon had never just been about pleasure and finding release. For her it'd been about connection.

Being with Damon had made her feel…not whole, because she'd always felt whole, but somehow more than whole, better than whole. She'd never known that such a feeling could exist. It'd taken her a long time to realise that feeling hadn't been mutual.

She glanced up. The darkness in his eyes, the guilt that swirled there, made her stomach clench. Pulling in a breath, she slowly let it out again. She had to get things back on track. She had to get things back to normal again. 'Okay, now we're even.'

'Even?'

'I lost control that night on the beach.' Her skin continued to fizz and spark. 'And now you've lost control here.' She managed to roll her eyes. 'But at least you found your control again.'

'Only because we were interrupted.'

'Then…then we'll be thankful for small mercies, right?'

But as they made their way back up to the main deck she didn't feel thankful. Not in the slightest.

They seated themselves at the ridiculously romantic table that had been set for them—all white linen and crystal—and stared at the amazing meal spread before them. 'Crab salad, lobster, artisan rolls and steamed vegetables,' she said, pointing to each dish. 'This looks amazing.'

'And vintage champagne.' He hefted the bottle in his hand.

'Mr Sorensen must really want you to buy one of his yachts.'

'I guess he must.'

She did what she could to get her raging hormones under control—a feat Damon seemed to have accomplished with barely any effort at all. Her back molars clenched. She could do this. She would make polite chit-chat if it killed her. 'Are you really in the market for one of these beauties?'

He shrugged. 'It could be fun, don't you think?'

'How much would one of these cost?'

'I'd put this one at twenty-five million, but I wouldn't want one this big.'

Her jaw dropped. He'd grown up poor, and she wondered what it must feel like to be so rich now, but she refused to ask a question so personal. She cleared her throat instead. 'I wonder who Mr Sorensen sells these too.'

As they ate, he regaled her with the names of the celebrities and princesses who made up Sorensen's clientele. He told her a funny story about a bidding war between two business rivals for one of these yachts. She understood exactly what he was trying to do. He was trying to dispel her tension. He was trying to make lunch as painless for her as possible. He was trying to distract her and take her mind off her worries and concerns.

The care he took with her now was the same care he showed her every day when he turned up on the beach with his surfboard—only speaking to her when she spoke to him; letting her set the pace and course of their conversations... Her mouth went dry.

It all spoke of... It all pointed to the fact that...

Did Damon still care about her? Or was she being fanciful?

In her chest, her heart turned a slow somersault. She did her best to ignore it. 'What does this all feel like? You had next to nothing growing up. You could buy one of these now if you wanted. Doesn't that feel amazing to you?'

So much for not asking personal questions.

He touched a white linen napkin to his lips. 'It should.'

'But?'

'But I don't give myself the time to enjoy it.'

Was it because of her? Because of how he'd earned his first big break?

He was showing her every kindness and consideration, and had done so ever since he'd arrived back in her life a month ago. He...cared for her. She couldn't deny that knowledge any longer.

It didn't mean he loved her. It didn't mean anything beyond the fact that he wanted her forgiveness. And even if it did mean more... She moistened her lips. She'd never give him a second chance and risk her heart to him again. *Right?*

But she recalled the way she'd flashed to life when he'd kissed her just then. Even now she could taste the euphoria, the delight... And the temptation kept circling through her.

Her heart started to pound. He'd told her he'd not been with a woman since her. That had to mean something. It had to mean something big.

Was she going to ask him why he'd betrayed her four years ago?

Or was she going to leave it all firmly in the past?

She glanced at him. While he had a lot of money, she had everything that mattered—a home, a community to belong to, a business she loved…and a grudge it suddenly seemed petty to keep.

She sat back and pulled in a breath. 'Fine, Damon, you win.'

He lowered his cutlery back to his plate. 'What do you mean?'

She gave up all pretence of eating. 'Why did you really betray me four years ago? Why was that grant so important to you? If you loved me—really loved me as you say you did—then the money shouldn't have mattered at all.'

Damon's heart pounded so hard that for a moment he couldn't catch his breath.

Was she prepared to listen to him?

What he was about to tell her wouldn't change a damn thing—it wouldn't change what he'd done—but it might give her a different perspective on the events of four years ago.

He'd always known, deep down inside where he knew the truth, that she deserved that from him.

'I mean, if you've changed your mind…'

Her shrug was nonchalant, but it didn't fool him. He knew the courage it'd taken her to ask the question. 'I haven't changed my mind. I'm just gathering my thoughts. You took me by surprise, that's all.'

He poured sparkling water into a crystal glass

and drank deeply. Sunlight glinted on the bay and waves splashed against the side of yacht. The beach glowed golden and mansions graced the headland in magnificence and splendour. But in his mind's eye he saw none of it. What he saw was the knocked-over garbage cans and trash that littered a dark alley and a doorway that led upstairs to the one-bedroom apartment he'd shared with his mother.

'I told you that I grew up in… Well, we weren't financially well off.'

'You said you were poor.'

'The truth is I grew up in inner-city squalor. My mother was a drug addict. There were times she turned tricks to get the money for her next hit.' His lips twisted. 'There were times I stole food because I was hungry.'

Her hand flew to her mouth and her eyes went wide.

'We lived above a Vietnamese bread shop owned by the Nguyens. They'd sometimes give me the leftovers at the end of the day. That kindness probably kept me out of juvenile detention.'

Eve pulled her hand away from her mouth. The pulse in her throat fluttered. It was all he could do not to lean across and touch his lips to it. 'I'm so sorry, Damon. I had no idea.'

Because he'd made sure nobody had any inkling about his background.

'That's an awful way to grow up.' With a visible effort, she swallowed. 'Two million dollars must've felt…it must've felt like a dream.'

His lips twisted. That kind of money had always seemed like an inconceivable sum. 'You want to know what I was really afraid of when I was a kid, Eve? Going into foster care. I know now I'd have been better off, but back then…'

He remembered the fear with a clarity he could almost taste—it'd been a dark, constant presence. It was why he'd done his best not to draw the attention of anyone in authority. His attendance record at school had been impeccable; he'd kept himself and his clothes clean; he hadn't got into fights or disrupted class. But it'd meant he had kept to himself. He'd never made the kind of friends he could invite home.

'My mother didn't really start going off the rails until I was seven. Seven through to eleven were the tough years.'

She blinked hard, but her gaze didn't waver from his. 'What happened when you were eleven? What changed?'

'Scott came into our lives. He was an old school-friend of my mother's and had been trying to track her down for an upcoming reunion. He told me later he'd always had a bit of a thing for her.'

'He became your stepfather?'

He nodded. 'He got my mother off the drugs, found us a place in the suburbs and got her a job—working in a clothing factory that made leisure wear. A factory full of women, so suddenly she had friends, and…' He was toying with a piece of lettuce, pushing it about his plate with his fork, and he lifted his head to meet her gaze. 'Hell, Eve, I can't tell you how good life was. I felt like we'd won the lottery. And then when I was fourteen Scott asked Mum to marry him and she said yes—and I felt like we'd won the lottery twice over.'

'He sounds like a wonderful man.'

'I hero-worshiped him.'

'Of course you did. He…he saved you. And he definitely saved your mother.' Her gaze turned uncertain. 'Is he still alive?'

A shaft of pain splintered his chest. 'He died a year ago. Cancer.'

She reached out and covered his hand. 'I'm so sorry.'

'Thank you.'

He stared at her hand, everything inside him throbbing. Almost without volition, he turned his hand over and laced his fingers through hers. And then held his breath. He had no right to touch her, to hold her to him—even just her hand. Especially after what had just nearly happened—and would've happened if they hadn't been interrupted. He'd nearly broken his word to her. *Again.*

Her grandmother was right—she was too good

for him. But she didn't pull away. A fine tremor ran though her—transmitted from her hand to his—but, with a tiny sigh she probably thought he couldn't hear, she left it there.

Gratitude rolled through him, fierce and fervid, and he had to fight the overwhelming and intense urge to tell her he loved her.

She didn't want to hear that. She'd moved on. He was here to do what he could to make things better for her, not worse. If he was lucky, at the end of this he might get the chance to call her a friend.

'Damon.' Her fingers tightened fractionally. 'Why didn't you ever tell me about your mother and Scott when we were together?'

He rubbed his free hand across his brow. 'When I was at university there was a girl I thought I was in love with. I took her home to meet the family…told her about my background.' He gave a low laugh. He'd been such an idiot. 'She came from a very nice upper-middle-class suburb and couldn't handle the grittiness of my childhood.'

'The insensitive…' She called her a name that made him laugh. 'You're better off without her.'

'I know that now, but at the time I was gutted. Scott and I talked about it and agreed it might be best if I didn't share details about my background with a lot of people.'

'Oh, Damon.' Her eyes went soft with sympathy and it made things inside him ache. 'Anyone with half a brain would've admired you all the more for what you'd overcome and what you'd made of your life.'

'We thought it might jeopardise my career chances.'

'So you got used to not talking about your childhood and family?'

He gave a heavy nod.

She was quiet for a moment. 'You thought I would treat you like your university girlfriend?'

It was hard to hold her gaze. 'I didn't know.'

Pain flashed in her eyes and he tightened his fingers about hers. 'Eve, when I first met you, you were engaged to Clay. Clay came from such a privileged background, and so did you.'

'But it wasn't on the same scale as Clay's,' she protested.

'No, but both your parents were professionals, and I knew how much pressure they were putting on you. And you have to remember how insecure I was. I hid it well, but when I compared myself to Clay…' He shook his head 'I couldn't work out what you saw in me.'

Her eyes widened, filling with tears, but then she swallowed and nodded. 'Okay, I can see that. You were wrong to short-change yourself, but given your background I can understand your insecurity.'

'I was scared too.' He wasn't ashamed to admit

it. Not now. 'I'd never loved anyone with the intensity I did you, and it scared the hell out of me. It made me sensitive—ridiculously so. And it made me a bit paranoid…suspicious.'

She leaned towards him. 'What do you mean?'

His heart beat hard. 'You and Clay broke off your engagement, but I sometimes wondered if the only person who knew about it was me. It wasn't shouted from the roof tops. It was kept pretty hushed up.'

'But you knew the reasons behind that. We didn't want to embarrass the company. Plus, our families were hoping we'd change our minds, so…' She shook her head. 'Clay and I knew it was over, though, and so did you. I figured that's all that mattered.'

'I knew what you and Clay had told me. But all the time a part of me couldn't help wondering if you were just having a bit of fun with me on the side and that you saw Clay as your future.'

'How could you think that?' She pulled her hand from his. 'I told you how much I loved you. *All the time*. I told you how much I wanted to build a life with you.'

He saw in that moment how much he'd hurt her, and he'd never loathed himself more.

'Why didn't you share any of this with me back then? Why didn't you talk to me? Damn it, Damon, all that time I thought I was building a future with you while you were waiting for it to break apart.'

'Not talking to you was the biggest mistake of my life.'

She pulled her arms in close to her body as if closing herself up...or preparing herself for a blow. 'That's why you threw me over for the grant.'

'No!' He dragged a hand down his face. 'Behind the scenes other things had started to snowball. And, yes, I should've told you about them—I see that now.'

Her shoulders unhitched a fraction. 'What things?'

'My mother...' Even now it was hard to push the words out.

Eve turned grey. 'She went back to drugs?'

He forced himself to laugh. 'Not quite, but it's evident she has an addictive personality. She took to gambling. Unbeknownst to Scott, she gambled all their money away. Now, that's an attractive family to marry into.'

'That's not what I'd have thought.'

'I know that now.' She'd never know how bitterly he regretted not confiding in her. 'Scott got her help—counselling. But he's proud, just like our Pru. He wouldn't let me help. I could've taken a mortgage out on a house for them, but he wouldn't let me.'

A breath left her. 'Until you were awarded that grant money.'

'No, not even then. Besides, this was all in the year prior to the grant.' He scratched both hands through his hair. 'Given some time and space, Eve, I'd have got over my inferiority complex and my insecurity—would have allowed myself to believe in your love.'

She glanced at him uncertainly. 'Okay.'

She didn't fully believe him, he could see that, but she was still willing to listen.

'But then Scott was diagnosed with cancer.'

For a brief moment she covered her face with her hands. 'I can't believe you tried to deal with this all on your own.'

'I was an idiot.' *Such an idiot.* 'Scott fixated on the grant. He told me he could die happy if I won it because he knew it'd mean I'd never face financial insecurity again…that I'd have the means to look after my mother.'

And *that* was why he'd betrayed her. Though, neither one of them said it out loud.

'If you'd told me all this at the time, I'd have taken my name out of the running.'

'I know that now too.' He swallowed back the bile that burned his throat. 'I returned to work one afternoon after having taken Scott to an oncology appointment earlier in the day. Mr Spelman called me into his office and asked me if I knew of any reason why he should award me the grant instead of you. I figured then that you'd won.'

'Idiot. He'd called me into his office earlier that same day and asked me the same question. If you'd swung by my office first, I'd have warned you.'

He stared at her. 'You're joking!' He'd always thought… 'What did you say?'

'I told him to toss a coin, because we were both as good as each other and that he couldn't go wrong either way.' She wrinkled her nose. 'It wasn't an answer that pleased him. It wasn't cut-throat enough.'

Neither of them spoke. He pulled in a breath. 'In the interests of full disclosure, Eve… I'm ashamed to say this…part of the reason I never confided my fears to you at the time is I'd have given anything I had to keep you in my life. And there was a part of me that was afraid you'd ask me to take myself out of the running for that grant so you could win it. I knew how much pressure your parents were placing on you. And if you'd asked it of me—even after Scott's diagnosis—I was afraid I'd do what you wanted.'

She stared straight back at him. 'I'd have never asked you to do that.'

'No, you wouldn't. But all I could see back then was how much I owed Scott. He'd been the one person in my life I could rely on.'

'You gave up what you most wanted to give him what he most wanted.' Her shoulders sagged.

'So that's why you hesitated the day I asked you if you regretted doing what you'd done. You couldn't actually say you regretted making Scott's final wish come true.'

'I hate what I did. But I can never regret giving Scott the sense of peace he needed. What is unforgivable is that I hurt you in the process.'

CHAPTER NINE

EVE STARED AT Damon and for a moment everything hurt. 'Why didn't you try and tell me all this at the time…or at least afterwards?'

He had to know it would've made a difference.

'Not only was I your social inferior, but I also saw myself as morally reprehensible. I'd never felt I deserved you. And, doing what I did, it was like I proved that to myself. When you said you never wanted to see me again, I figured getting out of your life was the best thing I could do for you.' His lips tightened. 'I became the morally bankrupt businessman I considered myself after that—cold, ruthless, unfeeling. I walked away from you and lost a part of myself.'

He'd hurt himself even more than he'd hurt her. 'If you'd told me all this four years ago, I'd have forgiven you.' For the first time she wondered if leaving Sydney had been a mistake. She'd handed in her notice and fled—she'd needed the space to lick her wounds and get over her hurt and humiliation in private. Walking away from the world of finance hadn't been a mistake. But maybe she should've given Damon a chance to try and explain.

'I didn't deserve forgiveness.'

She wanted to slam a hand down on the table and shout at him. 'What about what I deserved?'

He leaned towards her and everything inside her yearned for him. 'You deserved better than me.'

'And what gave you the right to decide that on my behalf?' Her insides screwed up tight. 'What is it with men? They think the little woman needs protecting and—'

'I never thought of you as the little woman, Eve.'

A seagull landed on the deck, squawking at them for leftovers. They both ignored it.

'I was screwed up, confused, not thinking straight.'

And he'd been grieving for the man he loved—she could see that. Her heart ached. But she also saw what he couldn't—he hadn't loved her enough to fight for her. She'd never been enough for her parents, and she hadn't been enough for Damon.

Her eyes burned and her throat ached. Ancient history. None of it mattered any more.

'But, when I saw you in that boardroom a month ago, I didn't want to be that morally bankrupt businessman any more. I wanted to be the man you once thought me.'

Things leapt inside her. She did what she could to pull them back into line, reminded herself that what he was telling her didn't mean anything in the here and now. They didn't have a future together. They hadn't had a future four years ago, and perhaps they had even less of a chance now. Their lives were so far apart. Damon would return to his corporate life and the bright lights of the city with his conscience eased, and she'd stay here in her gloriously low-key life where she belonged without the burden of an ugly grudge.

Win-win.

Only it didn't feel like a win. She felt like the biggest loser on the planet.

'Besides…' His smile didn't reach his eyes. 'If I'd done that, you wouldn't have all this.' He gestured at the bay—the sparkling water and golden sands, the sun shining down on it all. 'You said your life now is so much better than if you'd stayed in the city and the corporate world.'

It was.

And it wasn't.

'And this life suits you, Eve.'

She moistened her lips. She had nearly everything she wanted. Forcing her lips into a smile, she met his wary gaze. 'While you got on with things and made a success of your career, when all the odds were stacked against that.' He should be proud of himself.

Her words dragged a harsh laugh from him. 'I made a lot of money. But I stopped living. I stopped being who I wanted to be.'

He eyed her for a moment and then thumped his elbows on the table, a fist running back and forth over his mouth. It took a super-human effort not to let her gaze linger on that mouth and those lips.

'It's time for me to stop punishing myself and to start living again.' The knuckles on his fist whitened. 'What I need to know, Eve, is if you'll be okay with that.'

She jerked back, the spell broken. 'Of course I am!' What kind of person did he think her? 'I'd have forgiven you four years ago if I'd known the whole truth. And I forgive you now.'

He closed his eyes, his shoulders sagging as if released from a weight they'd been carrying for far too long. 'Thank you.'

He smiled then—really smiled—and she couldn't help smiling back, even though she wanted to cry. He looked so happy, and she'd helped him to find that happiness. She couldn't regret it. 'So...' She placed a dessert in front of him. 'Honey and chai *panna cotta*. Sounds delicious, doesn't it?' She had no appetite whatsoever.

'Eve, I'm not really hungry.'

She fixed him with her best boss glare. 'The Sorensens have gone to all this trouble.'

He eyed the dessert dubiously. 'So I'm going to eat the *panna cotta*?'

'*And* you're going to enjoy it.'

He laughed. She lifted a spoonful of dessert to her lips. Oh, the stuff was delicious! 'So,' she started, needing conversation, not wanting to let dark thoughts overtake her. 'What does this new life of yours look like? What's going to change?'

One gorgeously broad shoulder lifted and it was all she could do not to whimper. 'I've barely had a chance to think about it. I'm going to work less—much less—and delegate more. I know that much. My VP is currently in Frankfurt doing an incredible job closing a deal.'

He frowned, but he didn't look unhappy, just perplexed.

He gestured with his spoon. 'I'm surrounded by great people. I should be giving them more responsibility and a chance to shine without me constantly looking over their shoulders.'

Warm brown eyes speared hers. 'It seems to work for you at The Beachside.'

'I might be the overall manager, but I defer to Cassidy on anything related to the bar and restaurant because she knows her stuff. Same goes for my housekeeping manager.'

'It appears to work seamlessly.'

She shrugged. 'There's the occasional hitch, but we pull together when that happens and can usually fix it or come up with a temporary solution. So, yeah, it works most of the time.'

'And it frees you up to do the things that give your life extra meaning—like surf, and get involved in koala conservation, and...'

His face suddenly went so wistful, her heart started to throb. 'And?'

'Take the time to have a coffee and chat with people. You've made the time for friends.'

Oh, Damon.

'And you can now too,' she told him, refusing to let her sadness for him show. What a difficult life this man had led. 'You obviously have a knack for it.'

He blinked.

'Oh, for heaven's sake. For someone so smart you can be really dumb sometimes. Look how easily you made friends with Ron and his carpentry team on your first day here. And now both the Sorensens and the Daltons.'

'But...that's just business.'

'Only if you want it to be.'

His mouth opened, and then he closed it, as if turning her words over in his mind. As he did his eyes became brighter and his shoulders lost more of their hard cast.

'Believe me, you're not going to have trouble making friends.' She ate more *panna cotta*, suddenly hungry again. 'So, I surf and get involved in koala conservation. What are you going to do that you're passionate about?'

His gaze dropped. He stared out at the water and she didn't understand his sudden remoteness. 'Maybe I'll get a boat like this one. I have an apartment on the harbour with its own jetty.'

Wow. That sounded fancy.

She squinted out at the water too. What on earth was she thinking? He didn't need her help. He'd find his own way.

'I'm going to take a holiday.' He swung back, his eyes sparkling. 'Maybe I'll buy a holiday house in Mirror Glass Bay.'

She froze. *What?* That'd mean she'd be forced to see him…what…two weeks a year, maybe more? And every year she'd be forced to face the fact that he hadn't loved her enough. And never would.

'Scrap that.' The words ground from him as if he'd just taken a punch to the gut. His eyes lost their brightness. 'That's a daft idea.'

She shook herself. Where were her manners? Where was her *kindness*?

'Nonsense! It's a great idea. You'll always be welcome in Mirror Glass Bay. You've done so much for the town, Damon. You're one of us now.' How could she be so damn selfish? 'Everyone is very grateful for all you've done. You have friends here, and we'll always be happy to see you.'

'Everyone except you,' he said with a straight-forward candour that made her blink.

'Not true, I—'

'I just saw the look of absolute horror that passed across your face, Eve. You couldn't hide it.'

Her mind raced. She couldn't tell him the truth—that she still loved him...that she'd never stopped loving him.

How pathetic!

The only thing worse than his pity would be if he told her he loved her too in an attempt to continue making amends. She'd rather die!

'And you can't deny it now.'

'Fine.' She glared right back at him. 'It felt like a weird collision of my present and my past, and it felt confronting. I mean... God!' She threw up her hands. 'What if my parents show up next? But it was just a momentary thing and that weird moment has passed. My logical brain has kicked in again.' She forced her chin up. 'It'd be lovely to see you come back to Mirror Glass Bay year after year.'

'Liar.'

He said the word softly, but she sensed the anger that had built behind it. Anger she probably deserved. 'You've earned a place in the Mirror Glass Bay community, Damon—if you're not too afraid to seize it.'

'I'm not the one who's afraid.'

Maybe he was right, but she wasn't admitting as much.

'Besides, the deals you and everyone are counting on aren't sealed. Not yet.'

She gestured at the yacht and the luxury that surrounded them. 'My instincts tell me they are, and my instincts are still good.' She tried to pull the threads of her scattered mind together. 'I know you've bought those warehouses.'

'How the hell…?'

'And I know you're promising to fit them out to Sorensen's and Dalton's specifications. You're saving them time and trouble, which equates to money.'

He eyed her, looking as if he was doing his best to channel righteous outrage. 'Those were private deals!'

She waved that away. This was Mirror Glass Bay they were talking about. 'Don't worry, the details are private. What I'm saying is that you've paid whatever debt you imagined you owed me ten times over. You can live your life in whatever way you see fit without any thought to what I want or don't want.' She leaned across to drive her point home. 'I shouldn't be figuring in your considerations at all.'

He thrust out his jaw. 'Then you'd be wrong.'

She couldn't help it. Her heart leapt.

'I came here with one goal, Eve.'

Her mouth went dry. Hope wrung her from

the inside out. Was he going to tell her he stilled loved her? Was he going to say he'd come to Mirror Glass Bay to win her back? If he did…

Her heart thundered in her ears. If he did, she had a feeling she might just launch herself across the table at him. She couldn't hide what she felt any longer. Her heart pounded. For better or for worse, she loved Damon Macy.

'Do you want to know what that one goal was, Eve?'

She nodded. She couldn't speak. She couldn't take her eyes from his. After all this time, did they finally have another chance at love? What they'd had together had always been too big, too strong…too much to throw away.

It was why he hadn't been with another woman since her. It was why she hadn't been with another man.

'For four years I've been waiting for an opportunity to make it all up to you, Eve. I betrayed you, hurt you, and threw away the best part of my life. But helping you to shore up Mirror Glass Bay's future has meant I can finally pay my debt and give you something of real worth. I only wish I could've done it sooner.'

She stared at him, and slowly everything inside her collapsed and she laughed—watching herself as if from a long way away. Damon didn't love her. Maybe he had once, but now.

Kryptonite.

She was *such* an idiot. He saw her as an obligation, nothing more—a problem he'd needed to fix. While she was as big a fool as ever where he was concerned. He hadn't shunned other women because nobody else could live up to her memory. He'd been punishing himself.

While she'd been living some stupid half-life because she'd never been able to exorcise him from her mind.

Well, no more!

'I wanted to do something to make your life better, not worse.'

An obligation. A god damned obligation. Was there an uglier word in the English language? It was right up there with guilt and self-flagellation.

The hope that had gathered beneath her breastbone became a cold, hard lump that pressed on her heart until she could barely breathe. The kiss they'd just shared, that crazily intimate episode on the beach, hadn't meant anything. She'd been stupid to think otherwise. She'd been stupid to think that him showing up on his surfboard at the crack of dawn day after day meant anything either.

'You can tick that off your list, Damon. You've saved my community—you're providing it with at least two sources of industry that will translate to ongoing employment, all of which will lead to better infrastructure for the town. So, if you want to turn the Greamsman site into your ideal holiday house, feel free—you've earned it. Just don't forget to invite me to your house warming.' She didn't want to go to his god damned house warming!

She stabbed a finger at him. 'What I want you to do is to stop using me as an excuse from leading the life you want to lead.' While she was going to work on wrenching this wretched man out of her heart for good! 'You're welcome in Mirror Glass Bay—part-time, half-time, full-time, whatever you damn well please. Just as long as you realise that you and I are never going to be anything to each other ever again. We don't have any kind of future together. We're...*nothing*!'

His eyes widened at her anger. And then his mouth twisted and his face became dark, fire flashing from his eyes. 'Oh, don't worry, Eve. You've been crystal clear on that particular point.'

Good!

'That's one message I couldn't possibly mistake!'

'Good, because I wouldn't want to have to repeat myself.' She'd turned into a shrew, but she couldn't stop herself. 'I like my life exactly the way it is.'

'Oh, keep lying to yourself, Eve. Who knows, one day you might even believe it.'

What the hell...? He *couldn't* know.

'Four years ago, you ran away. And you're still running away now.'

'Not running away,' she managed through gritted teeth. 'Running to. Running to a better life, filled with people worth spending my time with.'

His eyes narrowed and the lines about his mouth deepened. 'And in the process you sacrificed your ambitions—because they scared the hell out of you. You can deny it all you want, but you came alive when we were working on ways to woo potential developers. You shone at that party—charming everyone and working towards several deals all at once. It filled your belly with a fire I bet you haven't felt in four years.'

She stared at him. He was wrong. Her mouth dried. 'You never needed me to save your town. You could've dusted off the skills you'd spent years at university learning and then perfecting at Spellman and Spelman, and you could've saved the town on your own.'

She shot to her feet. 'Oh, but why do that when it would've robbed you of the opportunity to come in and save the day? You swooped in too quick for anybody else to have the chance to make their mark.'

His head rocked back at her words and he shot to his feet.

'You've been wrapping up your reasons for being here in a nice, big, bright-red bow—*I want to make up for my shabby behaviour, Eve.* But, really, it's the thrill of the deal that matters to you. It's what's always mattered, what you've always loved.' More than he'd ever loved her. 'Regardless of the personal cost to yourself!'

His entire frame shook, and she watched it with a sick kind of fascination. 'You know what, Eve? It's finally occurred to me that you're right—we never really did know each other.'

She couldn't answer him, couldn't speak for the lump that had lodged in her throat.

His nostrils flared as he drew himself up to his full height. 'I vote we end this discussion right now.'

'Best idea I've heard all day,' she shot back.

Without another word, he spun on his heel and strode towards the back of the yacht. She blindly made her way to the front, only stopping when the railing halted her progress. She gripped the metal tightly until her hands ached with the same ferocity that made her eyes burn. Hauling in breath after breath, she told herself she wouldn't cry. She wasn't crying over Damon Macy ever again.

CHAPTER TEN

THREE NIGHTS LATER Damon found himself alone in The Beachside bar. He sat on a high stool at the bench that ran the length of the window at the far end of the room and stared outside at the darkness. A wind had whipped up and all the windows were closed to protect those inside. Low clouds scudded across the sky, hiding the glory of the stars he now knew sparkled behind them.

He scowled at the darkness and wondered if Cassidy would have a fit if he opened one of the windows just a crack to let the wind lash his face. He lifted his second glass of beer to his lips. Maybe it'd help him feel alive again.

Because, ever since that look of horror had passed across Eve's face when he'd tentatively proposed buying a holiday house here, something inside him had died.

He didn't deserve anything more, he reminded himself. She'd said she'd forgiven him—and the sympathy in her eyes when he'd told her his ugly story had been sincere—but it didn't mean she wanted him as a permanent or even semi-permanent fixture in her life.

The fight they'd had afterwards only reinforced that fact.

He'd still betrayed her. His actions four years ago, while mitigated by other circumstances, were barely excusable.

The Demon was reaping what he had sown.

With a bitter laugh he drained his beer in one long swallow. He should head back to his room and do some work—see how Owen was getting on. Except he didn't feel like doing any work.

And he didn't feel like going back to an empty motel room. For the last three mornings he hadn't gone surfing. He'd given Eve her space. They'd exchanged stilted but oh-so-polite apologies about losing their tempers and Eve had been assiduously pleasant to him ever since. He had a feeling he preferred it when she yelled at him. At least that had felt real. Even Dolores had abandoned him, as if she'd sensed the darkness of his mood and wanted to be away from it.

Still, he should never have kissed Eve. It'd made things too hot and heavy, frustrating and fraught. All of that tension had sparked their tempers.

He glanced up to his right. The flat above Reception was in darkness, which meant Eve was out somewhere, enjoying herself…living her life.

He glanced around. There were a couple of other tables still occupied. He wasn't keeping

Cassidy from closing. Striding up to the bar, he signalled for another beer.

Cassidy took his empty glass and slotted it into a rack beneath the bar. She pulled him another beer, not saying a word, but she raised a single eyebrow. She was a woman who could say a lot with just one eyebrow. Setting the beer in front of him, she leaned on her forearms. 'You look like crap, Damon. You coming down with something?'

The beer halted halfway to his mouth. Cassidy's solicitousness, brusque as it was, took him off-guard. 'I'm fighting fit.'

She snorted.

It took all his willpower not to fidget beneath her stare. 'Why'd you snort? What's so funny?'

'You said you were *fighting* fit. Doesn't look like you're fighting at all. Looks to me like you're surrendering—waving a big white hanky in the air and crying uncle.'

What the hell…?

He nodded at the bottles of liquor lined up on the wall behind her. 'You been sampling the goods?'

'Have you told her you love her?'

He froze.

Another speaking eyebrow made him swallow. 'So…not going to deny it, then?'

Denying it seemed wrong—like another Judas kiss—and he had no intention of wronging Eve ever again, whether she knew about it or not. But it didn't mean he was going to talk about it. 'None of your damn business, Cass.'

She straightened from her slouch. 'So you're in love with Eve, but you're not prepared to fight for her?'

'She hates me.' A strategic retreat seemed the best course of action.

'God, don't be so pathetic. Eve doesn't hate anyone.'

He dragged a hand down his face. 'You're right. But it doesn't mean she wants me in her life. And even if she did—' his hands fisted '—I don't deserve her.'

Cassidy stuck out a hip and folded her arms. 'So, for all your hero status in town, you're nothing but a faint heart.'

Her scorn stiffened his spine.

'She appears to have forgiven you, but you're too much of a mouse to win her back.'

'You're not hearing what I'm saying, Cassidy.' He ground the words out. 'She doesn't want me.'

'You know that for sure?'

He recalled the horror in Eve's face and it was all he could do not to flinch. 'Yes.' She didn't want him anywhere near Mirror Glass Bay, not even for a couple of weeks a year.

'A hundred per cent sure?' Cassidy persisted.

He went to say yes, and then out of nowhere he recalled Eve's earnestness when she'd told him he'd earned a place in Mirror Glass Bay. He scowled. 'Well?' Cassidy demanded.

'Ninety-five per cent certain,' he growled.

'So there's a five per cent chance you're wrong.'

He took a drink, pointing a finger at her when he lowered his glass again. 'Those are seriously bad odds.'

Her eyes narrowed. He had a feeling he preferred it when she raised an eyebrow. 'You're prepared to risk your money on a long shot, but not your heart…or your dignity?'

'This has nothing to do with my dignity!' He didn't give two hoots about his dignity.

His voice had risen and several people turned in their direction. He lowered it again. 'When I came to Mirror Glass Bay, I swore to only do things that would increase her happiness, not lessen it.'

'And you think pursuing her will make her unhappy?'

'Unwanted attentions,' he muttered.

'You let Eve decide if they're unwanted or not. You've no right to make that decision for her.'

Eve had said something similar to him on Sorensen's yacht.

'Anyway, that just sounds like one of those crap excuses men make when they're afraid of feeling vulnerable. If you're not prepared to put everything on the line for Eve, then it's better she forget about you.'

Did Cassidy think he had a chance?

Though, knowing Cassidy, she'd simply take great pleasure in watching Eve wipe the floor with him. Except they both knew Eve wouldn't take any pleasure in that. Cassidy was Eve's best friend. She wouldn't tell him to pursue Eve, declare himself, if she thought it would bring Eve pain or disturb her peace of mind.

He recalled that night on the beach when he'd worshipped Eve's body. There'd been magic in their kisses, in the heat of his caresses, and in her temporary surrender to the pleasure he could give her. So much magic, it'd left him reeling and had sent Eve into a spin—and she'd retreated, fled.

That kiss on the Sorensen yacht had been magic too. But...was he the one fleeing this time?

He recalled the mornings on the beach when he'd been struggling with his surfboard, when Eve—as if she couldn't help herself—would tell him to try moving higher up his board, or to speed up his paddling to get onto a wave properly. They'd only been tiny scraps of advice, but she'd still taken the time to give them to him when she hadn't had to.

Five per cent?

'Five per cent is crap odds.'

'Then I'd make my gesture a big one, if I were you.'

The next morning Damon tucked his surfboard under his arm and made for the beach. The wind was still up, and high, grey cloud masked the sun, but it hadn't rained. And he figured it wouldn't much matter if it did. He was going to get wet either way, right?

Eve, wearing a pair of black trousers and a long cardigan, intercepted him in the park before he reached the path down to the beach. 'What are you doing?' she demanded.

He stared at her. 'Why aren't you in a wetsuit?'

She looked great in a wetsuit—sleek, lean and strong.

She looked great out of a wetsuit too. She looked great in anything.

'You're not surfing?' He couldn't keep the disappointment from his voice.

'Have you actually looked at the surf this morning? Spared it a passing glance from your balcony on your way down?'

Um... He'd been in too much of a rush to get down to the beach—to see her. He'd hoped bobbing in the sea for a bit, and admiring her skill on a board, would help him come up with a plan, provide him with inspiration for a big gesture.

Eve gestured seaward. 'Oh, Grasshopper, you have much to learn.'

He followed the direction of her hand and swallowed at the churning mass of ocean that greeted him. That wasn't the kind of sea one bobbed around in.

'That, my friend, is a dangerous surf, and not

for the likes of beginners.' She followed his gaze and added, 'The guy on the yellow board is currently ranked three on the Australian circuit, while the guy on the white board is a former Argentinian champion. They have the experience to deal with these kinds of conditions.' She glanced at him again. 'You really want to go out in that?'

He shook his head and turned back towards the motel. 'You ever surfed seas like that?'

'A couple of times, but I didn't enjoy it.' She glanced back behind them. 'I only risk swimming in seas like that when there are a lot more people around.' She stopped then and stared right into his face, her eyes serious. 'You can't ever take the ocean for granted, Damon. Always check the conditions before you go in. And, if in doubt, don't.'

Wise advice for surfing. It was often wise in business too. But Cassidy was right—it was the wrong approach to love. He loved Eve—with everything he was—and he'd find a way to show her and convince her of his love. And maybe, just maybe, if he were lucky, she'd take a chance on trusting him again.

'Go put your board away and come have some breakfast. There's something I'd like to run by you.'

And then she was gone, and he was racing upstairs to his room to get changed like an eager fourteen-year-old getting ready for his first date.

* * *

'I ordered us both a full English breakfast,' Eve said when he slipped into the seat opposite. 'I hope that's okay.'

'Sounds perfect.' He studied her face. 'What's on your mind?'

She blew out a breath, her gaze sliding away for a fraction of a moment before returning. Worry spiked through him. 'Has something gone wrong with the Sorensen or Dalton deal?' If it had, then he should be the first one to know. But Eve had access to some kind of bush telegraph that gave her an inside scoop well before everyone else. 'Or have you heard back from the Environmental Protection Agency?'

'How would I know? I thought you were handling all of that.'

'Yeah, but you seem to hear things a good eight hours before I do.'

That made her laugh, lightening her eyes and easing the weight in his chest. 'Rest easy, Damon. I haven't heard anything to the contrary.'

Good.

'What I want to talk to you about is—' her gaze slid away again '—me.'

His absolutely favourite topic of conversation. He sat a little higher in his chair. 'Okay.'

'But first… Damon, that fight we had—'

'You don't have to say anything.'

'I want to.'

He stilled and then nodded.

She kept her gaze trained on his. 'I want you to know I didn't mean the things I said. I'm honestly grateful for everything you've done. I was angry because...' Her gaze dropped and she shrugged. 'Because four years ago you didn't confide in me, and it seemed that we lost so much when we didn't have to. But it was childish of me to lash out like I did, and I'm sorry.'

'While I lashed out at you because I was angry at myself.' He grimaced. 'The height of maturity, I think we'll both agree.' She huffed out a laugh and he found his lips lifting. 'I'll accept your apology if you'll accept mine.'

'Done.' She bit her lip and held out her hand, looking adorably uncertain. 'Friends?'

He shook her hand, things inside him clenching. 'Friends.' He eased back and tried to still the hammering of his heart. 'Now, what did you want to talk about?'

She moistened her lips. 'I've been thinking about what you said to me on the Sorensens' yacht. About it maybe, possibly, being a mistake to have turned my back so completely on...on my training.'

He studied her carefully. She looked neither peeved nor resentful and he let out a slow breath.

Cassidy chose that moment to set two plates piled high with food in front of them. 'Enjoy, folks.'

They thanked her, and Damon lifted a piece of toasted sourdough to his mouth. Before he bit into it, he said, 'We were both a bit het up—emotions were running high. I'm sorry if I overstepped the mark.'

'I don't know about overstepping the mark. What I do know is that you hit it dead centre—you hit a big, fat bullseye.'

The toast dropped back to his plate.

'You were right—I have missed it. And I didn't even realise it until you pointed it out.' She shook her head, as if appalled at her own cluelessness.

'Understandable. You've had a lot on your plate.' It was all he could do not to reach across and clasp her hand.

'I suppose.'

'And I think you equated the ruthlessness and ugly cut-and-thrust of a few people within the corporate world with the entire industry.'

'I don't want to go back to that world full-time.' She gestured around. 'This is my life and my home.'

'But?'

She suddenly leaned towards him. She hadn't touched her breakfast yet. 'Do you think I could make a tiny little investment firm here in Mirror Glass Bay work? I'm thinking of only one or two days' worth of work a week. I don't think there'd be the demand for anything more than that, but...what do you think?'

'You're asking my advice?'

She picked up her fork and speared a mushroom, before setting the fork back on her plate, mushroom untouched. 'It's just, I've been out of the game for four years.'

'Garbage.' He tried to hold back a grin. 'I've seen you reading the financial pages while you sip your coffee. I've seen people in here ask you what you thought about certain stocks and shares.'

'That's just small stuff. Nobody's paying me—it's just an opinion.'

'An opinion backed by experience and a savvy business sense, Eve.'

She met his gaze. 'I trust your advice on this, Damon. You have one of the shrewdest heads in the business.' And then she outlined her plans for a small investment firm, just servicing the local community, and explained how she thought it might work. He sat there and listened, his heart starting to sing. 'Well?' she finally demanded.

He wanted to lean across and kiss her. Well, okay, he always wanted to kiss her. But he specifically wanted to kiss her in this particular moment because she'd come alive.

Her courage made his heart leap. She was facing her fears and was pushing through them to create a solution and find a way forward. She was amazing. He wanted to tell her she was amazing, but it would come out too intense—too much too soon. So instead he grinned, and she blinked, as if dazed. 'You already know it's a brilliant plan.'

She pondered his pronouncement and then shook her head. 'No. I thought it was an okay plan, but not brilliant. It's why I wanted to run it by you.'

'It's better than okay—it's a great plan. But there's one thing you haven't considered.'

She leaned towards him, so close he could count the spattering of freckles across her nose. 'What?'

'Expansion.'

'Oh, I don't think—'

'In time it *will* become a full-time gig.' Clients would flock to her. 'If you don't want to do it full-time, you need to think about attracting good staff.' She'd be crazy to think otherwise.

Without letting her gaze drop from his, she called Cassidy over. 'Hey, Cass, would you be interested in becoming a partner in The Beachside?'

'In a heartbeat.'

'Want to discuss it over pizza tonight?'

'Can't. Remember?'

Eve slapped a hand to her forehead. 'That's right! Well, what are you doing in a couple of hours, around ten?'

'I'm pencilling in a meeting with you,' Cassidy said, before heading back to the counter to take an order.

'What are you doing tonight?' He hadn't meant to ask, but the question slipped out.

She sent him a smile that made his heart beat faster. 'Big plans. I hope you're free.'

'I am.' He'd be whatever she wanted him to be. If he'd had plans, he'd have cancelled them.

'I seem to recall that you used to like poker.'

'I still do.'

'Well, I've organised a poker night. Here. Tonight.'

He glanced around in search of a flyer.

'It's invitation only.'

Something in her tone had him swinging back to face her.

'I wanted to apologise for making you feel so bad the other day on the yacht, Damon. For making you feel you weren't welcome here. You'd be a great asset to Mirror Glass Bay. And tonight, at the poker game, you're going to see exactly how well you fit in.'

She grinned at him and determination solidified in his gut. His five per cent suddenly felt like seven, or maybe even ten, per cent. 'I can't wait,' he said, finally starting to attack his breakfast—now cold—with gusto. It was the best damned breakfast he'd ever eaten.

CHAPTER ELEVEN

EVE FINISHED THE last of her breakfast and set her knife and fork into a neat line on the plate before blotting her mouth with a paper napkin and glancing at the man opposite, so acutely aware of him it almost hurt. Damon only had a few more days in Mirror Glass Bay—the auction was this coming Saturday night—and after that he'd return to Sydney with its bright lights, his apartment on the harbour, his business…and with the past firmly behind him.

She told herself she was glad for him. He'd carried a burden of guilt these past four years that was entirely out of proportion to his crime.

She cringed again at the memory of the way she'd flown off the handle at him. Her hurt had got the better of her, and it made her want to die a thousand deaths. All he'd been doing was trying to put things right. After the childhood he'd had, and all the difficulties he'd had to battle, the one thing he hadn't deserved was her anger and resentment.

She was only grateful he hadn't realised the true reason behind that hurt and anger.

She had an urge to order another entire full English breakfast, but she suspected it had nothing to do with hunger and everything to do with comfort—an attempt to plug the aching gap that yawned through her.

Get over yourself.

They were saving her town; she was going to embark on an exciting new business venture; she'd learned the truth about the past and it helped to know she hadn't been some sucker Damon had manipulated for his own ends. She was surrounded by friends. It was time to draw a line under the past and move on.

She pulled in a breath and sent Damon a smile. 'Thank you for listening to my plans—for letting me pick your brain—and for being so encouraging. I just took unashamed advantage of you and...' She trailed off with a shrug, not sure what she was trying to say.

One corner of his mouth hooked up in a wicked smile that tilted her world to one side. 'You can take advantage of me any time you want, Eve.'

She swallowed. He almost sounded as if...he was flirting with her!

Oh, don't be absurd. That was just wishful thinking.

Outside the wind had died down but it had started to rain—a gentle, nourishing patter that the local farmers would welcome, not to mention The Beachside's gardens.

'I appreciate that more than I can say.' She smiled to hide the sadness circling in her chest. 'I was really awful to you when I first saw you again in Byron Bay.'

'It was a shock. You hadn't been forewarned. And you had every reason to loathe me. It was understandable.'

He'd tensed, but someone who didn't know him as well as she did wouldn't have noticed. His eyes didn't leave her face and it made her mouth dry. 'I was wrong, Damon, and I'm sorry I made you feel so bad.'

'Eve, I—'

'You're the best thing that could've happened to Mirror Glass Bay—a thousand times better than Greamsman and his resort. You've poured money into this place that you didn't have to. And you're not going to get a high return on your investment.'

Those whisky-brown eyes suddenly gleamed. 'You never know. Maybe I will.'

She went to clasp his hand, but at the last moment pulled back. If she touched him, he'd know—he'd sense how she felt about him—and she wasn't putting that kind of pressure on him. She wasn't taking advantage of any lingering guilt or sense of obligation he might still harbour. She moistened her lips. He followed the action and everything inside her clenched tight. 'Thank you, Damon. Truly—thank you for everything you've done.'

Things throbbed behind his eyes that she couldn't identify and didn't understand. 'What would make Mirror Glass Bay perfect?' he finally asked.

Him. He would make Mirror Glass Bay perfect. Not that she could say as much.

'Sealing the Sorensen and Dalton deals, which you tell me are nearly in the bag. I don't need anything more than that.' *Liar.* 'Mirror Glass Bay doesn't need anything more than that.'

He nodded, but not in agreement. More as if he were pondering something imponderable.

'That kind of local industry will keep our primary school and medical centre open.' And that was all she'd wanted to achieve. 'Your conference centre will be a boon for The Beachside and local eateries if you decide to go ahead with it.'

His lips curved upwards. 'Not to mention a boon for my staff.'

And maybe it'd mean she'd get to see him once in a while. 'And the boss, if he decides to take some time out of his busy schedule,' she said, desperately hoping she didn't sound as if she was fishing.

He nodded, but didn't commit himself. 'What else would make Mirror Glass Bay ideal?'

She pushed on to hide her disappointment.

'Oh, I don't know. Maybe a research centre for Beck. She could do good things here. We need to conserve and preserve what we can where we can, and she's on top of all the latest research, so…' God help her, but she'd still rather he built a holiday house in Mirror Glass Bay than for Beck to get her research centre or for his employees to get their corporate beachside retreat.

'And?'

She stared at his raised eyebrow. 'And nothing. This place is perfect the way it is.' But he raised his eyebrow even higher. She didn't want to dwell on the intriguing planes of his face or the faint shadow accenting his jawline, so she searched her mind for things to add…*anything*! 'Okay, then, to get my little investment company off the ground without a single hitch.' There'd be hitches, of course, there always were… 'I'm excited by that.' She loved running The Beachside, but it didn't have to be either-or. She could do both. And somehow that seemed the perfect solution.

'Eve, Eve, Eve.' He shook his head in mock disappointment. 'All of those things are so predictable. Go wild, let your imagination soar.'

Oh, right. They were playing *that* game—if she found a genie in a magic lamp…if money and resources were no object.

She leaned back and let her creativity take

flight. 'Okay, it'd be beyond fun to hold an annual surf competition here.'

'Hell, yeah. I'd come to see that.'

Excellent. What else would he come for? Maybe an annual poker competition. *Don't be an idiot.* That'd be laying it on too thick.

'What else?' he urged.

'Anything I want?'

He nodded.

'This is utterly indulgent, but I'd love it if there was a little boutique in town that sold cute dresses and shoes, funky jewellery...'

'Handbags,' Cassidy said, coming up to clear away their plates and obviously catching enough of the conversation to want to play along. 'And a hairdresser,' she added. 'They wouldn't need to be open every day of the week, just one or two.'

'Ooh, and a spa—facials and massages.' Eve sighed.

A dreamy expression crossed Cassidy's face. 'A bit of waxing, tinting and fake tanning.'

They both raised their hands at the same time and wiggled their fingers. 'Manicures.'

Damon leaned back and stared at them. His grin hooked up the right corner of his mouth, making her want to swoon. She shrugged, suddenly self-conscious. 'You told me to dream big.'

'In that case,' Cassidy said, balancing plates, 'add a bus-load of hot, eligible men to that list.'

Eve and Damon laughed at the staged look of

longing that crossed Cassidy's face as she walked away. Eve shook her head. 'But we can live without those things…or make a trip into Byron Bay for them.'

His expression sobered and his eyes searched her face. 'Isn't there something you want—something just for you?'

Him. But she couldn't say that out loud.

'What do you want for yourself in the long term?'

She'd barely let herself think about it. 'I…'

When she hesitated, he shifted a fraction on his seat. 'Do you want to keep living in your tiny flat above Reception?'

She gripped her hands together beneath the table. 'We're dreaming big, right?'

'Absolutely.'

'Then one day I'd like to buy a house somewhere along Marine Drive with a beach view and a good back yard for a dog. I'd like to have a dog.'

She'd like to have a family too—a husband and kids—but she couldn't think about that. Not while she was looking at Damon. She'd never be able to think about that until she met a man who touched her the way he did, and she didn't even know if that was possible.

'That sounds…nice.'

Had she imagined that wistful note in his voice?

He suddenly stood and clapped his hands together. 'I better get a kick on—there are some things I need to do.'

She swallowed as he walked away. His old life was pulling him back already. She hoped he meant what he'd said to her that day on the yacht—that he'd make time to have a life outside of the office. He deserved one. He deserved to be happy.

'You look stunning!'

Cassidy's wide-eyed approval helped to bolster Eve's nerves as she strode into the restaurant wearing a satin cocktail dress in fire-engine red. Maybe it was perverse, but she wanted Damon to see her, to notice her, wherever he might be in the room tonight.

She smoothed a hand down the chiffon overlay, fingering the satin band that tied into a square bow beneath her breasts. 'Not too much?'

Cassidy shook her head. 'It's perfect.'

'You're not looking too shabby yourself.' Her friend was poured into a midnight-blue number that was fitted from collarbone to mid-thigh and then flared out around her knees and calves. 'Can you breathe in that?'

'Just about,' she said with a wink.

Eve had a feeling that quite a few men this evening would have trouble catching their breath when they caught sight of her.

'The band are setting up,' Cassidy said. 'I still don't know how Damon managed to get them—the man's a magician—but they're such a draw-card. We're going to have a heck of a crowd tonight.'

Both women took deep breaths and Cassidy said, 'Looks like our first guests have just arrived. Ready?'

Eve went to nod, but Damon chose that moment to walk in wearing a dinner jacket and white tie and her tongue stuck to the roof of her mouth.

Beside her, Cassidy let out a long, low sigh. 'Your Gran called him a two-million-dollar gigolo…said he wasn't worth that kind of money.'

She'd what?

'But, looking at him now, I'm not so sure.' Her friend winked at her. 'I'm thinking you'd pay that price twice over.'

Eve snapped upright. Was she that obvious? Cassidy sauntered off towards the waiting staff lined up behind the bar before Eve could make any reply. And then Damon stood there, lifting her hand to his lips, his eyes warm with masculine appreciation. Her heart crested a wave and then hurtled down it with dizzying speed.

'You look beautiful.'

'So do you.' He didn't let go of her hand, and warmth radiated from where his lips had touched her bare skin. He moved in closer, bending down as if to whisper something in her ear, but a burst of laughter from the doorway as the guests started to arrive had him easing back. She reclaimed her hand and sent him a tight smile. 'Let the fun begin.'

When she'd found out the band Damon had organised, she'd known they'd draw a crowd, but it exceeded even her grandest expectations. The bar and restaurant became so crowded people spilled into the gardens and onto the footpath outside the motel. Eve was grateful she'd had the foresight to hire big outdoor heaters. Winter was balmy here, but the nights could still be cold and crisp—especially in a cocktail dress.

She glanced around and shook her head. Mirror Glass Bay had just put koala conservation on the map. *Go, Mirror Glass Bay! And thank you, Damon Macy.*

When the band finished playing their opening set, Damon chose that moment to move to the makeshift stage. 'We have a few minors here tonight who all have to leave by nine o'clock and I promised them we'd announce the winner of the raffle before they left. Eve, do you want to come on up here and draw the name of the winner for this top-of-the-line surf board from Joey's Surfhouse? The one-stop shop for all your surfing needs.'

She hadn't known he was going to ask her to draw it. He should've asked one of the Sorensens or the Daltons. She so wanted Pru to win! She wouldn't be able to hide her disappointment if it went to someone else. Pulling in a breath, she made her way to the platform. 'Good luck, everyone,' she said, but she stared straight at Pru as she said it. The hope in the young girl's face tugged at her.

Crossing the fingers of her left hand behind her back, she reached inside the tombola barrel and pulled out a ticket. She handed it to Damon, but he gestured for her to read it. She unfolded it, stared at the name and her jaw dropped. A big lump lodged right in her throat. She held the ticket out towards him, wanting proof that she wasn't dreaming.

He read the name, grinned and then spoke into the microphone. 'And we're delighted to announce that the winner is… Pru Atkinson!'

A big cheer went up. Pru stared up at them in open-mouthed shock before giving a huge squeal of delight and hurtling up on stage to hug both of them and collect her prize.

'Please tell me you didn't rig that,' Eve murmured to Damon later. 'We sold something ridiculous like seventy books' worth of tickets.' He wouldn't have…

Would he?

His eyes danced. 'How many books did you buy?'

'Ten.'

'And who's name did you write on each of the tickets?'

'Pru's, of course.'

'Cassidy bought a book and did the same. Ditto for your gran. And so did Pru's mum.'

'But that still only accounts for thirteen books. I mean, I know it helps to increase the odds, but only slightly, and—'

'I bought fifty books.'

She did a double take. 'You did what?'

'So that's sixty-three books all in Pru's name.'

She wanted to hug him.

'That *really* helps the odds.'

She wanted to hug him and never let go.

'Look, the auction is about to start.'

They turned, but before they could move closer Granny Beth blocked the way. Dear God, had she really called Damon a two-million-dollar gigolo?

Before Eve could usher her away, Gran fixed Damon with an unblinking eye. 'Mr Macy, my granddaughter has fully explained to me the circumstances surrounding the events four years ago. Now, Eve has a big heart—bigger than mine, it must be said—but I wanted to acknowledge that I might've been a little harsh in my words to you the other day. I'm prepared to reserve judgement for the time being and give you a chance to prove me wrong.'

His jaw dropped. 'I...um...appreciate that.'

'I like what you've done for the town.'

'Thank you.'

With a nod, she held out her hand. He shook it, and then without further ado she turned imperiously on one heel and marched away.

He picked up his jaw to stare at Eve. 'Did you put her up to that?'

She shook her head. *But...wow.* 'I think you can take that as an official seal of approval.'

Damon ushered Eve—the most stunningly beautiful woman there tonight—to the side of the room where they could watch the auction unhindered.

While the band was an undeniable hit, the auction also exceeded expectations. He glanced around at the excited faces of the Mirror Glass Bay residents that he'd come to know and care about...people like Ron and his team of carpenters, Beck and Cassidy...but his gaze kept returning to the flushed face of the woman he loved. Eve.

All evening, unbeknownst to her, she'd captured his entire attention, had held him in thrall. Oh, he'd chatted and laughed with other people, had even danced with Cassidy and a couple of other women, but the entire time he'd ached to be with Eve.

Except...every time she glanced at him her smile faded.

He did that to her—he dimmed her light.

Somehow, and without meaning to, he sucked the joy from her life. And every single time her smile faded it was like a knife sliding in between his ribs.

The ten per cent chance he'd given himself to win her heart dwindled to one thousandth of a per cent.

But he was still going to prostrate himself at her feet. It didn't matter how slim his chances. He wasn't leaving Mirror Glass Bay without knowing for sure, without knowing he'd given it his all.

Both Eve and Cassidy had chided him for making assumptions. He had no hope—couldn't help assuming Eve would be glad to see the back of him—but he wasn't acting on that assumption. She would get the choice. He'd leave his fate in her hands. The risk of humiliation didn't matter in the face of such a prize—a lifetime with the woman he loved.

When the band stopped for their penultimate break, he strode up to the microphone. Amid cheers, he thanked everyone for supporting the koala conservation project. He announced the official sum raised. And then he paused. The room hushed, as if it could tell from the expression on his face that something of great moment was about to take place. He waited until Eve stilled and glanced up, meeting his eyes across the crowded room.

He would not be a faint heart. Not this time.

'A lot of people made tonight happen, and I want to thank each and every one of you. I started on a journey here to help improve Mirror Glass Bay's local economy because of Eve. It's her love and passion for this town that has made things happen. And I want to make a couple of official announcements in relation to Operation Mirror Glass Bay. First, two very respected local businessman—Garry Sorensen and Simon Dalton—will be moving branches of their existing businesses to the industrial site on the edge of town. The final contracts were signed yesterday.'

A big cheer went up.

'In addition to that, on the old Greamsman site two new initiatives are underway. The first of these is Beck Daniels' much-yearned-for research centre. It'll be small to begin with, but there'll be the potential for expansion, which we're hoping will attract government grants. The research centre will be located on the north-western side of the site. On the rest of the site, I'll be building a small boutique conference centre.'

An excited murmur went about the room, but he was barely aware of it. He couldn't drag his gaze from Eve's face, her eyes wide and vulnerable as she stared at him.

He knew she was grateful for all he'd done and was doing. And in all likelihood she'd be appalled when she found out why he'd done it—

because he still loved her. He had a speech prepared for that eventuality too, so she wouldn't blame herself and feel bad for hurting him. Something along the lines of the fact that he couldn't think of a more worthy way to spend his money than safeguarding Mirror Glass Bay's financial future.

He hoped to God he wouldn't have to use it.

His hand clenched about the microphone. He probably would. And he *would* find the strength for it.

'With this influx of new industry, the local infrastructure such as schools and medical centres should actually improve rather than decline. The likelihood of Mirror Glass Bay now becoming a ghost town is almost zilch.'

Another big cheer went up, even from those people in the room who weren't local residents. 'And I wanted to celebrate that in a special and memorable way. Eve once joked to me how much fun it'd be if the town could host a surfing competition. Through the week, I spoke to the National Surfing Board, and we've agreed to a five-year sponsorship deal. In September next year, the very first Mirror Glass Bay Surf Festival will take place.'

Eve's hands flew to her mouth—in shock, he suspected—but they couldn't hide the way her lips widened into a huge smile or the way her eyes started to dance.

He spared Cassidy a glance. 'Cass, I think that will also answer your special request.' A town full of hot, eligible men!

She grinned and sent him a thumbs-up.

'I've also been in negotiations with a hair-dresser-cum-beautician who's interested in a sea change. Yesterday I took her through several houses that are for sale in town and she's settled on a place on Beach Road that she thinks will make the perfect home business.'

Eve's hands dropped back to her sides and she shook her head, wonderment shining from her eyes. A smile rose through him. Regardless of whether she loved him or not, he had this moment and the knowledge that, in the end, he had helped to improve her life rather than ruin it. In this moment he'd made her happy.

'I was reliably informed that a hairdresser, beautician and manicurist would make many of the women in Mirror Glass Bay very happy, and I'm a guy who likes to deliver.'

Laughter rippled around the room. Someone called out, 'Three cheers for Damon,' and the cheers that followed nearly lifted the roof.

Damon gestured for quiet. 'It's not me you need to thank—it's Eve. She's been the driving force behind all of this.'

And then Eve was moving towards him, and his throat closed over, and he could barely draw breath. She nudged him out of the way so she could speak into the microphone. 'Damon, as usual, is being ridiculously humble. None of this could've been possible without his perspicacity, his determination and—'

She broke off to meet his gaze and the sincerity in her eyes threatened to unbuckle his knees at the same time as it fired his blood.

'And his kindness,' she finished.

It didn't mean she loved him, but... 'Eve's wrong.' He spoke into the microphone again but his eyes never left hers. 'I'm just the man who's determined to do whatever will make her happy—who's one goal in life is to do exactly that.' His mouth went dry. 'The man who wants that job for the rest of his life.'

Her mouth opened and closed, and then she leaned towards the microphone again. 'And now you're all going to have to excuse us. The band are back for their next set so...um...enjoy.'

And then she seized Damon's hand and led him out the nearest door into the gardens, which were littered with people cooling off, taking a little couple time or simply enjoying the fresh air. Eve shivered and he immediately shrugged out of his jacket and slipped it about her shoulders.

'Your role is to give me whatever I want?' she whispered, her eyes huge in her face.

He nodded.

A thread of humour briefly lit her eyes. 'Do you think you could find us some privacy?'

He knew the perfect place. Taking her hand, he led her along Marine Drive with its glorious beach views. Partway along, he veered them down a path and onto the beach. She let go of his hand, kicked off her sandals and sank her toes into the sand. Only then did she meet his gaze again. 'What you said back there, Damon.'

'I meant every word.'

She moistened her lips. 'It sounded a lot like you were saying that you…'

'That's exactly what I was saying.' He reached out and touched her face, just the backs of his fingers to her cheek. 'I love you, Eve. I've always loved you. I never stopped loving you.'

Uncertainty raced across her face. And vulnerability. His heart started to race. Did he see hope there too? He leaned towards her. 'You don't believe me?'

'I don't *not* believe you. I just…' She hesitated, her hands clenching and unclenching. 'What I'm wondering is, if you've sensed how I feel about you, and in your misplaced guilt are trying to give me what I want…'

She wanted…*him*?

'But, Damon, you have to understand that you don't owe me anything. And certainly not a sacrifice like that. Just because I love you doesn't mean—'

He didn't wait to hear any more. He swept her up into his arms and claimed her lips with his.

kissing her with all the hunger in his starved soul. She seemed to bow under the onslaught, but flung her arms around his neck, held tight and kissed him back with a matching hunger.

They eased apart several long moments later to gulp oxygen into starved lungs, holding onto each other to keep their balance, to keep from falling.

'That,' Eve gasped, 'wasn't a pity kiss.'

His heart thundered in his ears. 'I feel a lot of things for you, Eve, but pity isn't one of them.' He cupped her face. 'Please say it again.' He was begging, gut-wrenchingly needy, but he couldn't help it.

She didn't laugh at him. She didn't tease him. She didn't even smile. She stared deep into his eyes and he recognised the tenderness reflected there. 'I love you, Damon. I love you so much it frightens me.'

'You don't need to be frightened. I'm never going to hurt you again. I promised.'

She nodded.

'I nearly made the same mistake now that I did four years ago. I nearly left without telling you how I feel—because I don't deserve you. I know that, but...'

'But you gave me a say in the matter.'

He wanted her to know that he'd listened, had taken her words on board when she'd told him how she felt and how his actions had made her feel. 'It only seemed fair to give you the chance to reject me.'

She reached up on tiptoe to press a swift kiss to his lips, and it sent fire licking along his veins. 'That was never going to happen. Also, just for the record, you do deserve me—every bit as much as I deserve you.' She suddenly frowned. 'What on earth made you think I would reject you anyway?' She shook her head, as if she couldn't fathom how he'd ever come to that conclusion.

'Every time you looked at me tonight the smile disappeared from your face and your eyes went dark, almost haunted. I know you said you'd forgiven me, but I figured no matter what you said you couldn't forget what I'd done.'

She smoothed her hands across his chest. 'No, Damon, it was because I was in a hundred different kinds of agony tonight knowing that tomorrow you'd be out of my life for good. I didn't know how to bear up under that knowledge and keep my happy face on. And you'd been beating yourself up so badly for what happened four years ago, and were so determined to made amends, I didn't feel I had the right to tell you I still loved you. I thought you'd stay because it's what I wanted, not because it's what you wanted.'

He'd read the situation so appallingly inaccurately that he made a silent resolution then and there never to keep anything from her again.

A smile, tremulous and beautiful, trembled on her lips. 'But you are staying, aren't you, Damon?'

A sunburst of something pure and joyful shot through him. He turned her to face the road. 'See that house there? I bought it this week.'

She clutched his arm. 'That house has the best beach view in the entire street. How did you convince Molly Collins to sell?'

'I made her an offer she couldn't refuse.' He glanced down at the woman by his side, something inside him taking flight at the expression on her face.

She grinned up at him. 'You really are staying.'

It hit him then—she didn't care about that house or the view. She cared about *him*.

His throat thickened. He swallowed. 'I'm staying.' He was going to turn that house into Eve's dream home. He didn't tell her that, though. There would be time for that later.

'What about your work?'

'I plan to become a master delegator. I want to work remotely. I'll probably need to fly down to Sydney for a day or two here and there.'

'I… I could come with you.' She laughed at whatever she saw reflected in his face. 'Only if I won't be in the way, of course.'

'You'll never be in the way.'

'I just want to be where you are.' She slid one warm hand across his cheek. 'Where *you* are is my home. If you need or want to live in Sydney, then—' she shrugged '—I can do that.'

Would she relocate for him? The realisation stunned him. He knew how much she loved this place. He'd started to love it too. He'd never ask her to leave. Her generosity, her kindness, the size of her heart cast him adrift and reeled him in both at the same time.

Concern shone from her eyes. 'What is it? What's wrong?'

'Nothing! I just... I don't deserve to be this happy.'

Her face gentled. 'Yes, you do. You really do.' She lifted her chin. 'You said your role in life was to make me happy, right?'

'And I stand by that.'

'Then I want the first item on that "making Eve happy" agenda of yours to be for you to understand that you deserve to be this happy. And to cherish being this happy. You work hard, Damon, and you're good to people. And I love you. I have good sense and good taste—I'm not a stupid woman.'

'Of course, you're not!' Pity help anyone who suggested otherwise!

'Then trust my judgement.'

He stilled.

'Please?'

Slowly he nodded. 'I'll try.' Because he did trust her but, more than that, he wanted nothing to mar her happiness, and that included his own insecurities.

Solemnly he put her away from him and went down on one knee, pulling out the velvet box that had been burning a hole in his pocket all evening. 'Eve, I love you. I want to spend the rest of my life with you. Will you please marry me and make me the happiest man on the planet?'

He opened the box to display the champagne diamond nestled inside.

She glanced with trembling wonder from him to the ring. Her bottom lip trembled, she clasped her hands to her chest and his heart swelled, because he could see her answer plainly in her face.

And then she did a double take. 'Damon!' She stared at him, scandalised. 'What did you do? Walk into the jewellery store and buy the biggest diamond you could?'

He grinned. *She was going to say yes!* Maybe not right now…she might insist on a long engagement. And he didn't mind. She could have whatever she wanted. But she'd told him she loved him. She wanted to be with him as much as he wanted to be with her.

'Not the biggest—the prettiest,' he corrected. 'The colour and brilliance of this stone reminded me of you. Eve, your soul shines as brightly as this diamond. We can change it if you don't like it.'

If possible, her expression became even more scandalised. 'We'll do no such thing!'

If possible, his grin widened. 'Is that a yes?'

She pulled him to his feet. 'Of course that's a yes. I love you, Damon.'

He kissed her then, and it was a long time before either one of them spoke again.

* * * * *

*If you enjoyed this story,
check out these other great reads from
Michelle Douglas*

The Maid, the Millionaire and the Baby
Miss Prim's Greek Island Fling
The Million Pound Marriage Deal
A Baby in His In-Tray

All available now!